SPIDER-MAN:

CONTENTS

FOREWORD: 4

CHAPTER ONE:
SUNDAY IN THE PARK WITH VENOM 5

CHAPTER TWO:
STALKING FEAT 32

CHAPTER THREE:
ELLIPTICAL PURSUIT 58

CHAPTER FOUR:
THE BONEYARD HOP 80

TRUCKSTOP OF DOOM 103

SPIDER-MAN: VENOM RETURNS™ Originally published in magazine form as THE AMAZING SPIDER-MAN #'s 330, 331, 332, 333, 344, 345, 346, 347 and THE AMAZING SPIDER-MAN ANNUAL #25. Published by MARVEL COMICS, 387 PARK AVENUE SOUTH, NEW YORK, NY, 10016. Copyright © 1990, 1991, 1992, 1993 Marvel Entertainment Group, Inc. All rights reserved. The AMAZING SPIDER-MAN, VENOM, and all prominent characters appearing herein and the distinctive likenesses thereof are trademarks of MARVEL ENTERTAINMENT GROUP, INC. No part of this book may be printed or reproduced in any manner without the written permission of the publisher. Printed in the U.S.A. ISBN #0-87135-966-9. First Printing: March, 1993. GST #R127032852

10 9 8 7 6 5 4 3 2 1

CREDITS

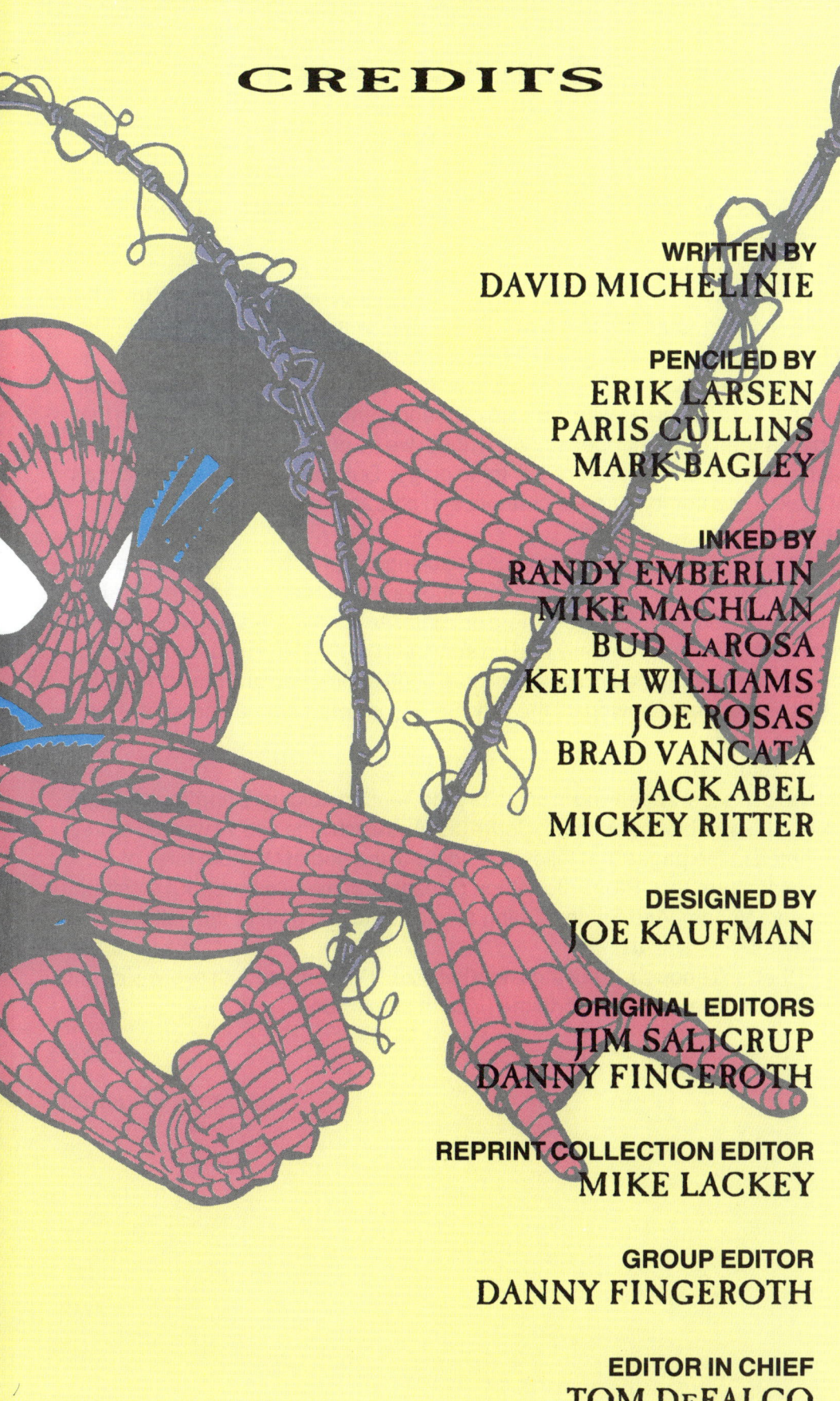

WRITTEN BY
DAVID MICHELINIE

PENCILED BY
ERIK LARSEN
PARIS CULLINS
MARK BAGLEY

INKED BY
RANDY EMBERLIN
MIKE MACHLAN
BUD LaROSA
KEITH WILLIAMS
JOE ROSAS
BRAD VANCATA
JACK ABEL
MICKEY RITTER

DESIGNED BY
JOE KAUFMAN

ORIGINAL EDITORS
JIM SALICRUP
DANNY FINGEROTH

REPRINT COLLECTION EDITOR
MIKE LACKEY

GROUP EDITOR
DANNY FINGEROTH

EDITOR IN CHIEF
TOM DeFALCO

FOREWORD

Sometimes you know why things work. Sometimes you don't. But the fact remains: they work.

So it is with Venom.

Sure, readers had liked Spidey's living costume that he brought home from the Beyonder's world. Sure, people had loved David's writing and Erik's art. Just like they had loved David's writing and Todd's art. Sure, everybody enjoys stories about vengeance-bent psychopaths. But who'd've thought when you put them all together...you'd come up with this kind of phenomenon?! It's the kind of thing that can't be planned. It just happens. Every month we do our best to come up with the thing that'll make comics history. We try to plan it. But nobody really understands what makes one combination of creators and characters click. But the fact remains: they do.

Venom started as a mysterious figure reaching out of nowhere to push Peter Parker out a window or in front of a roaring subway train. He's ended up as one of Marvel's most popular characters, hero or villain. And, while we always figured the living costume would eventually end up some sort of continuing character in Spidey, we never imagined it'd be even more popular on a bad guy than on a good one. But our readers showed us the way. So Venom went from a one-shot villain to what he is today.

Venom returned.

Instead of his just appearing in one storyline, fandom told us: Bring back Eddie Brock and his symbiotic soulmate. So we did. And each time you've wanted more.

Reprinted in the pages that follow are some of the coolest Venom tales of all. They also feature Styx, Stone, Jonathon Caesar, and many others. But mostly they feature Venom. And Spidey. Going at each other in some of their all-time great battles.

And if that isn't enough, just watch how the size of Venom's mouth evolves from issue to issue. That alone is worth the price of admission.

Enjoy,

Danny Fingeroth

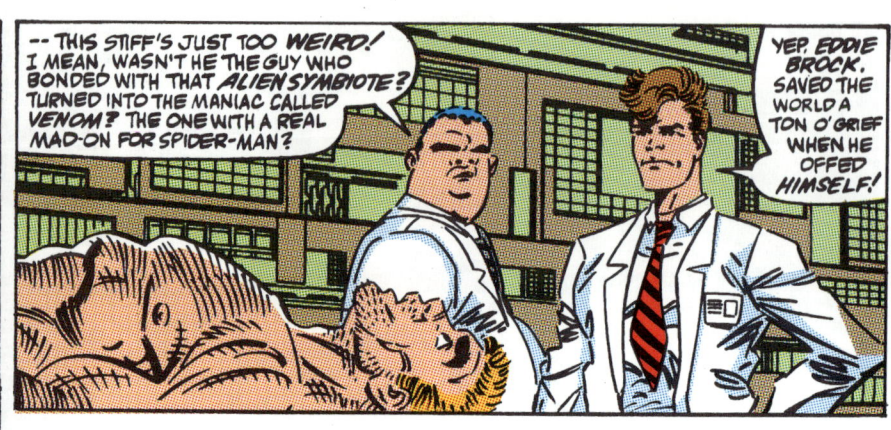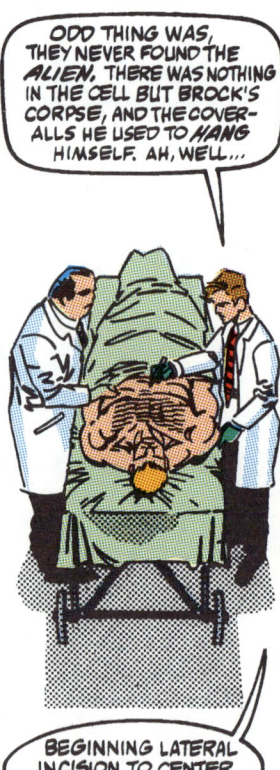

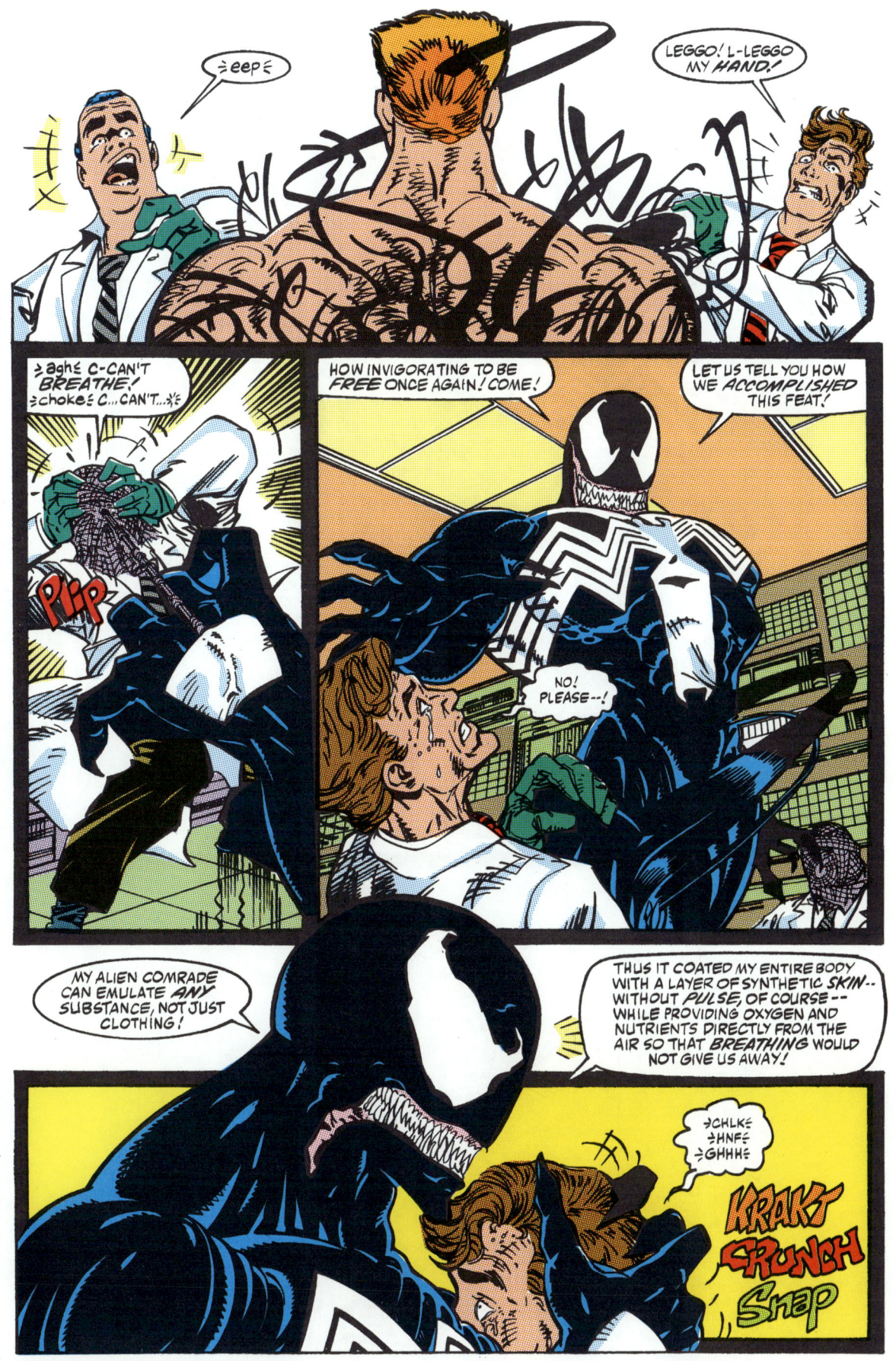

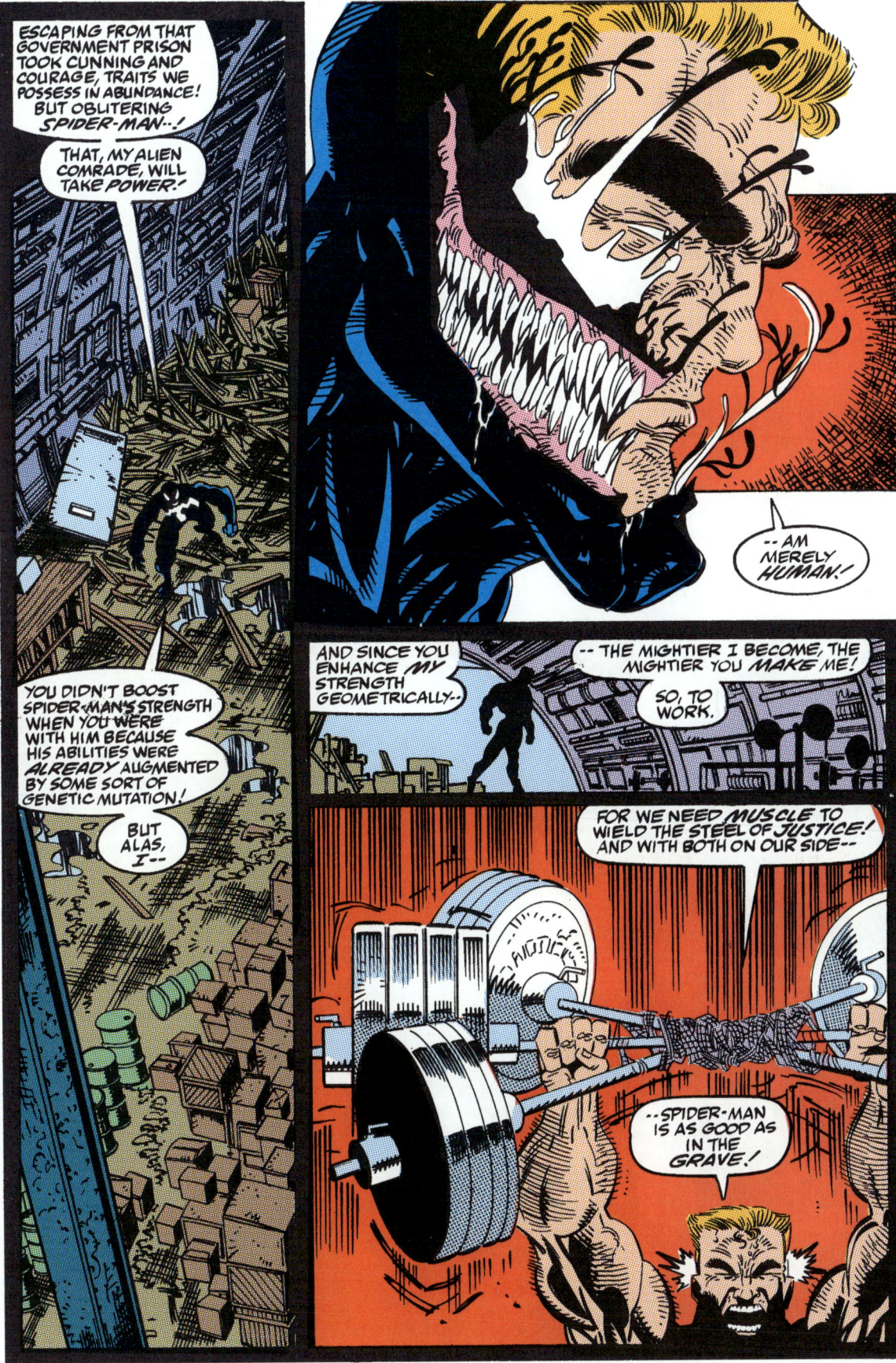

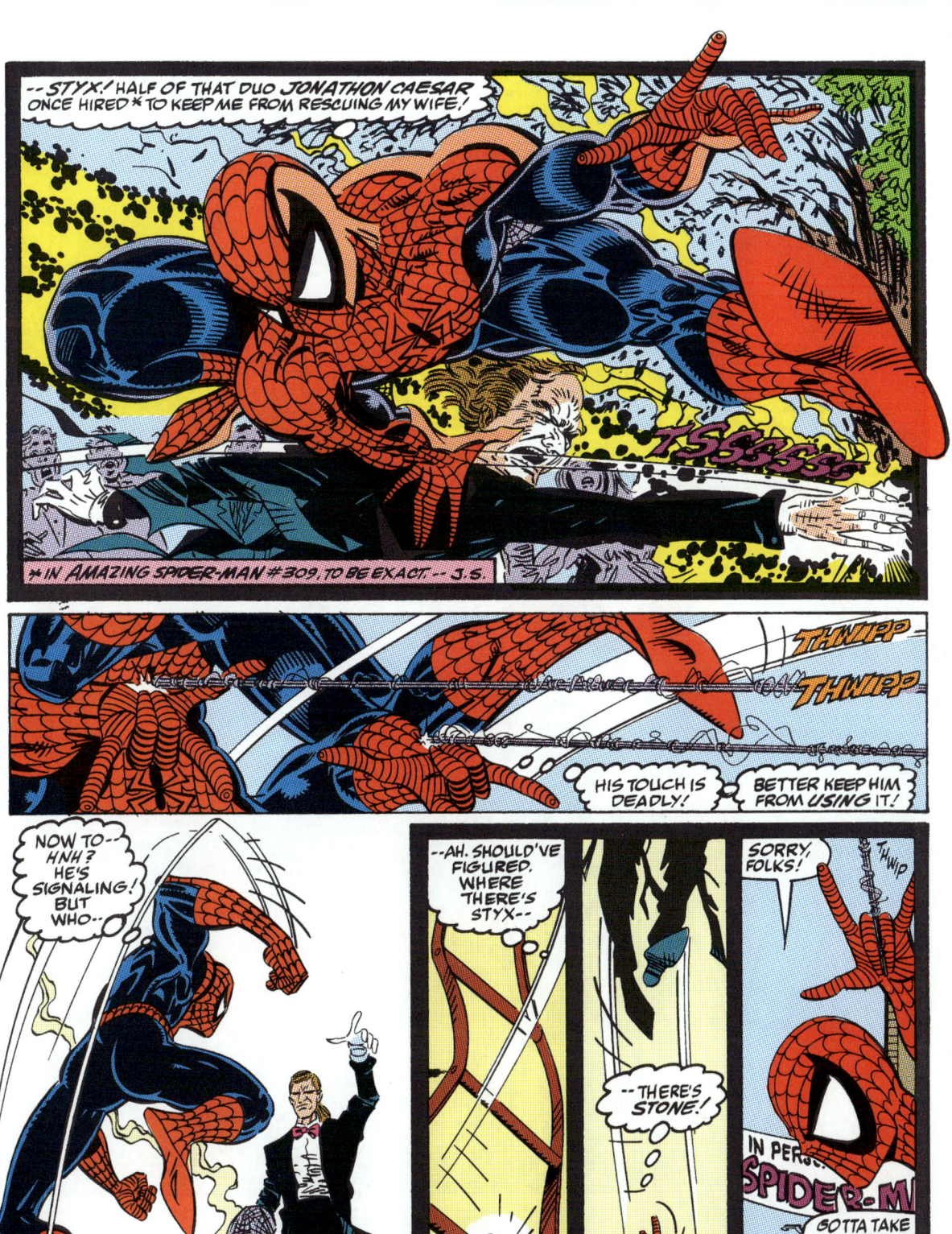

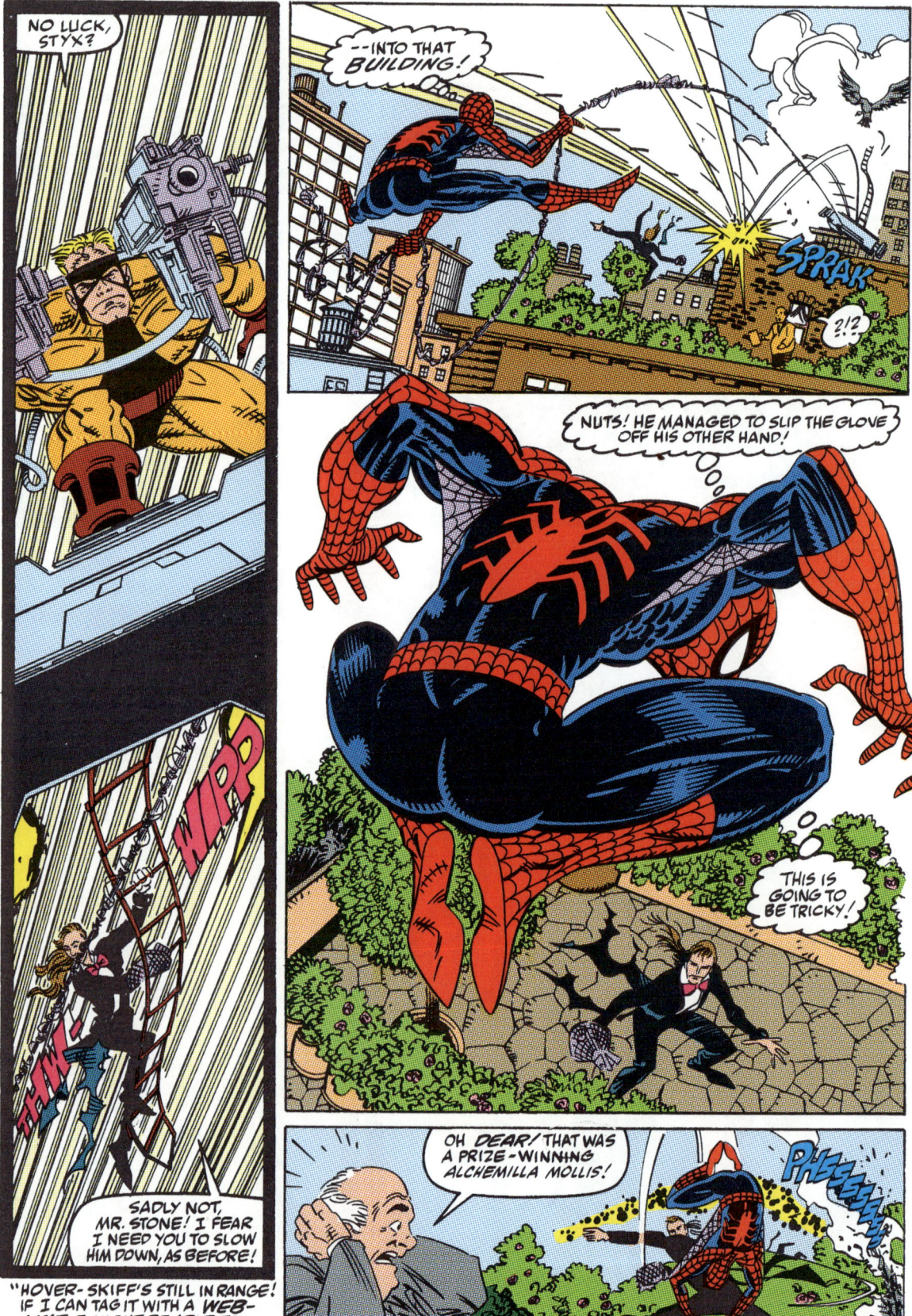

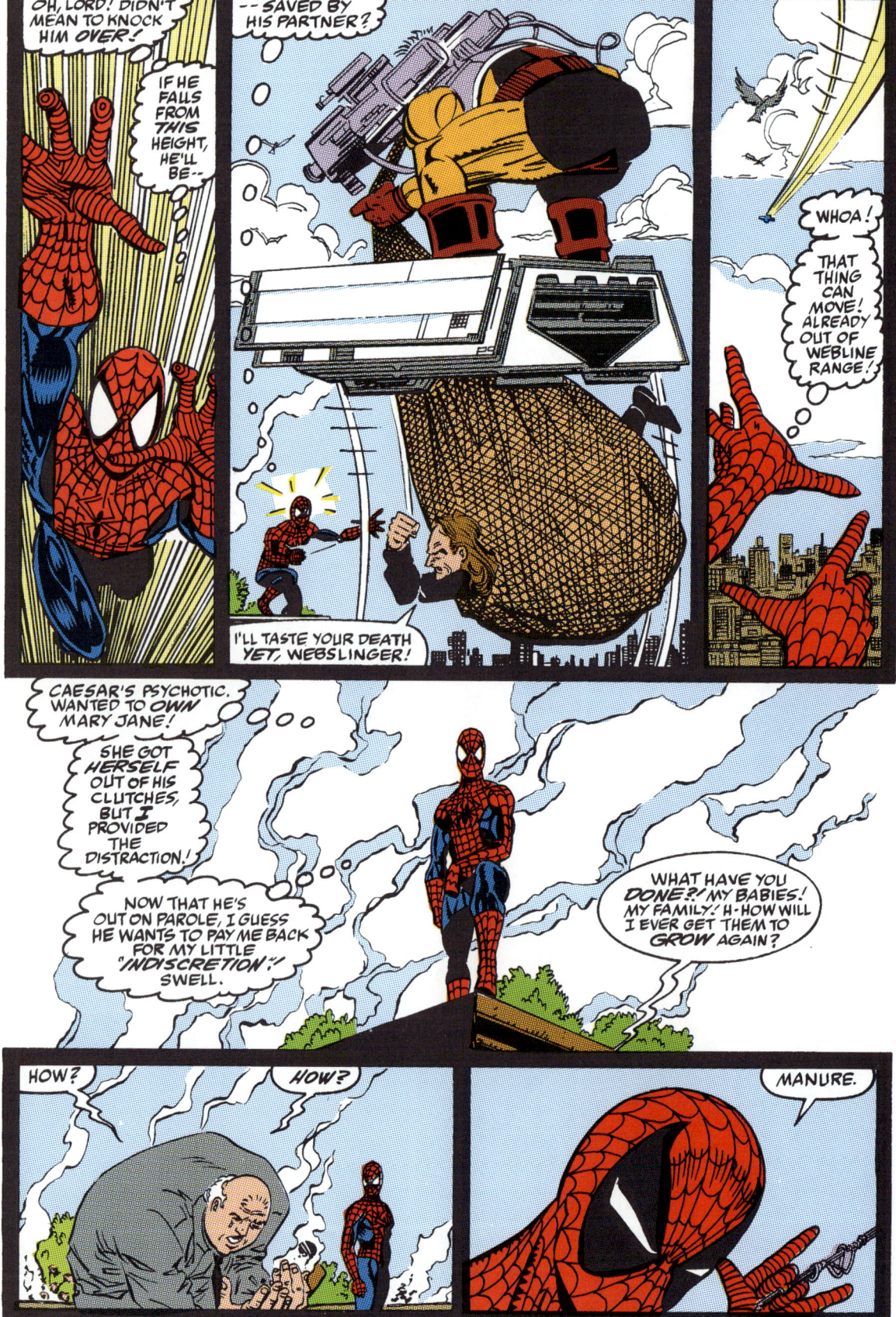

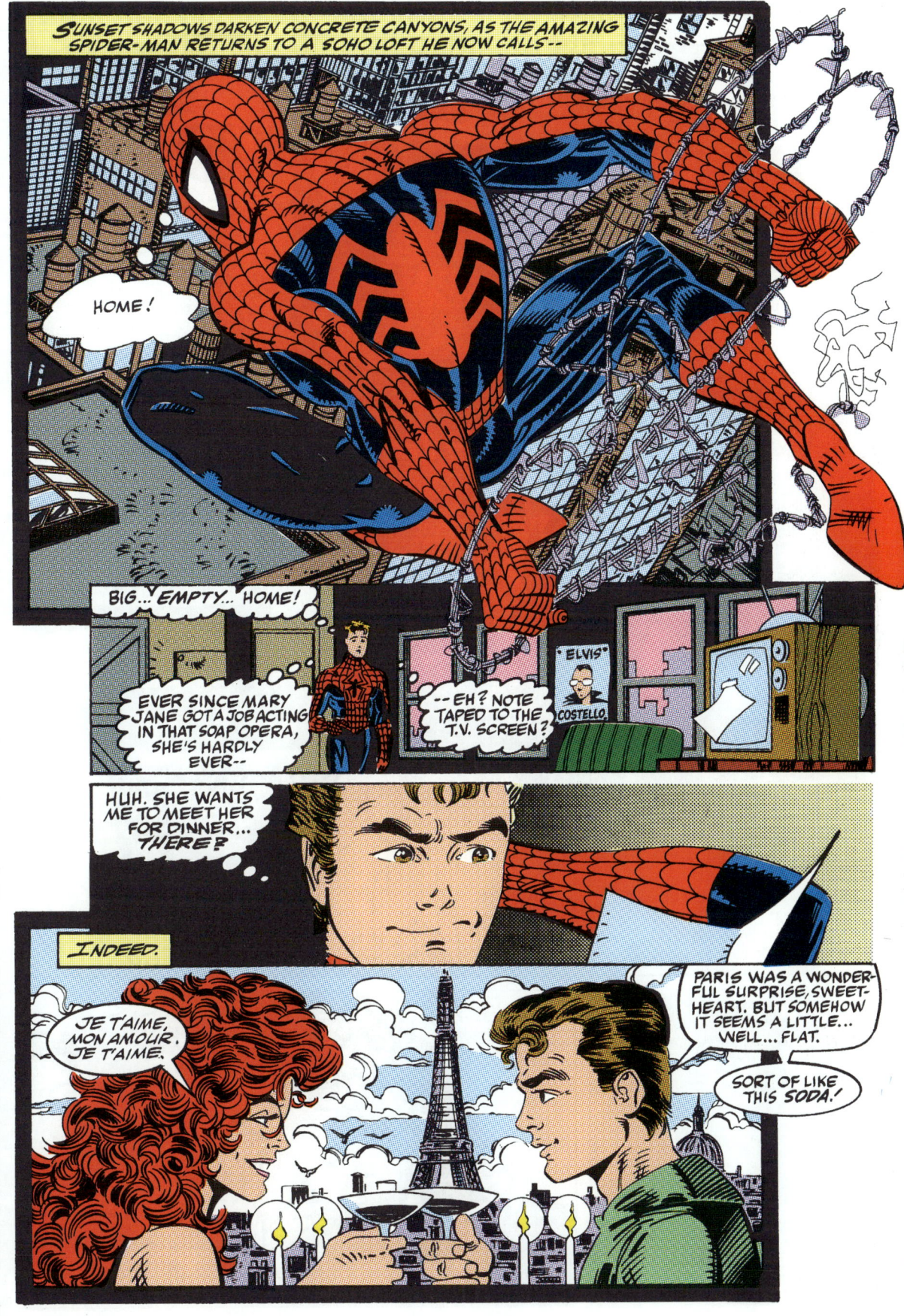

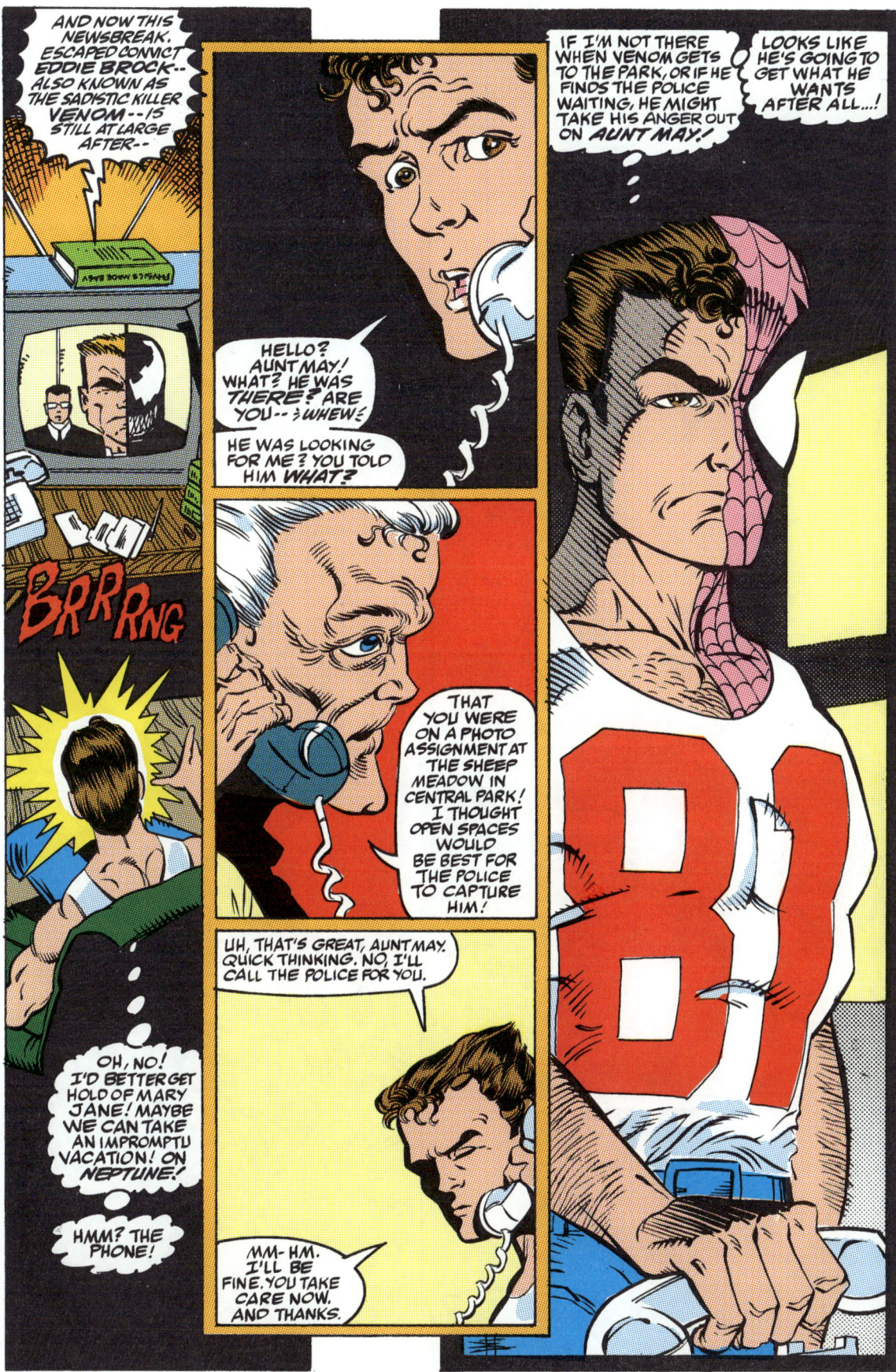

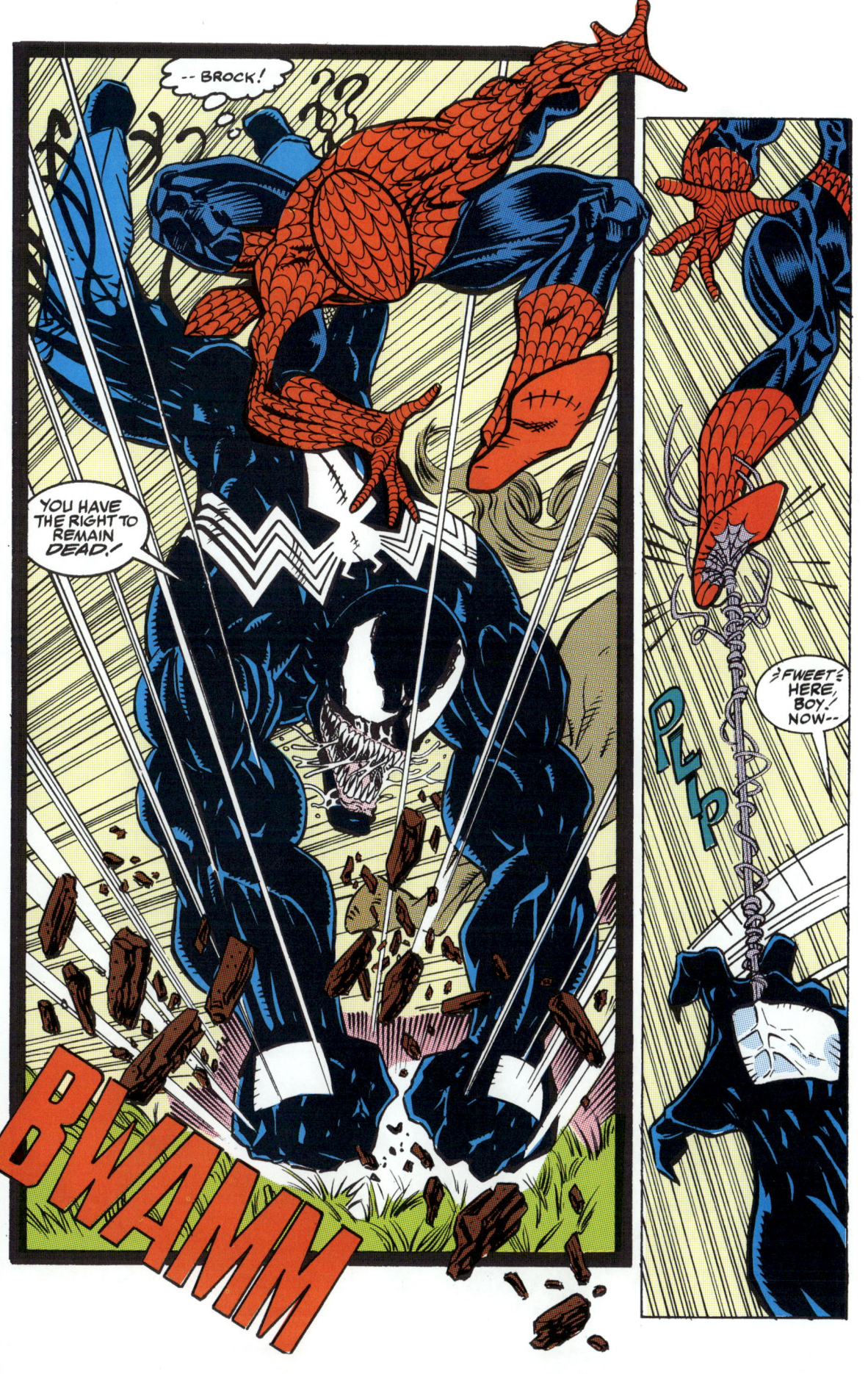

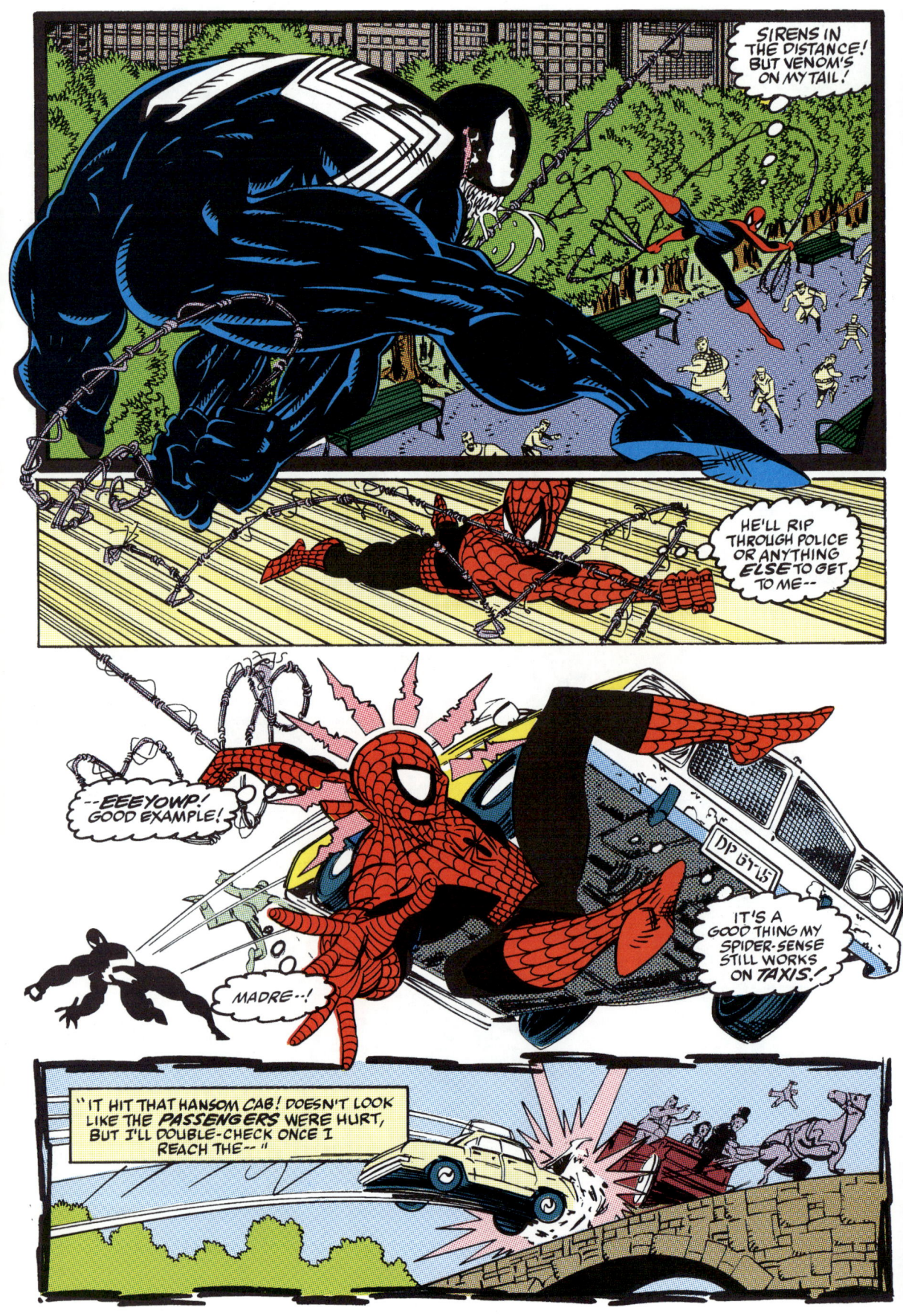

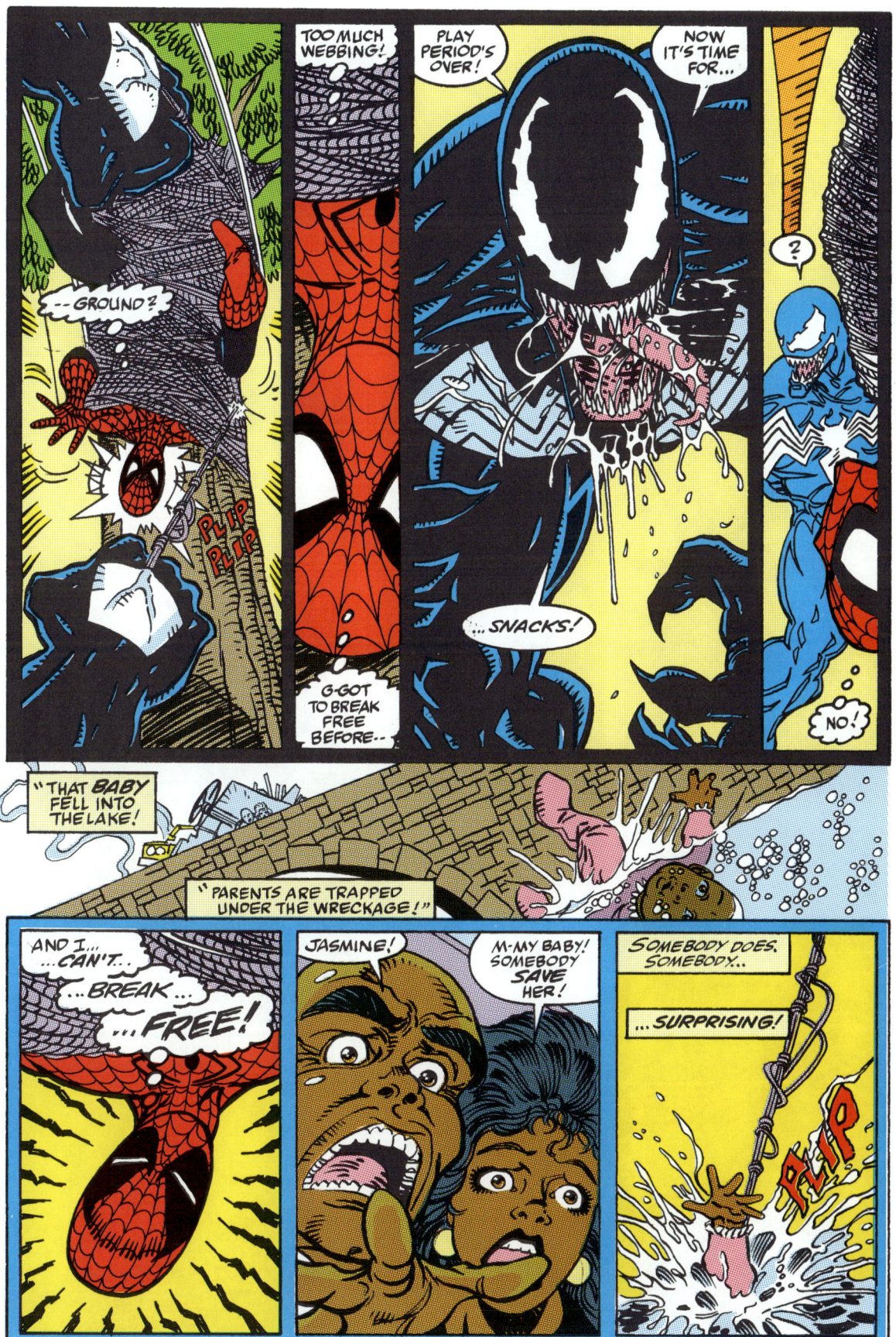

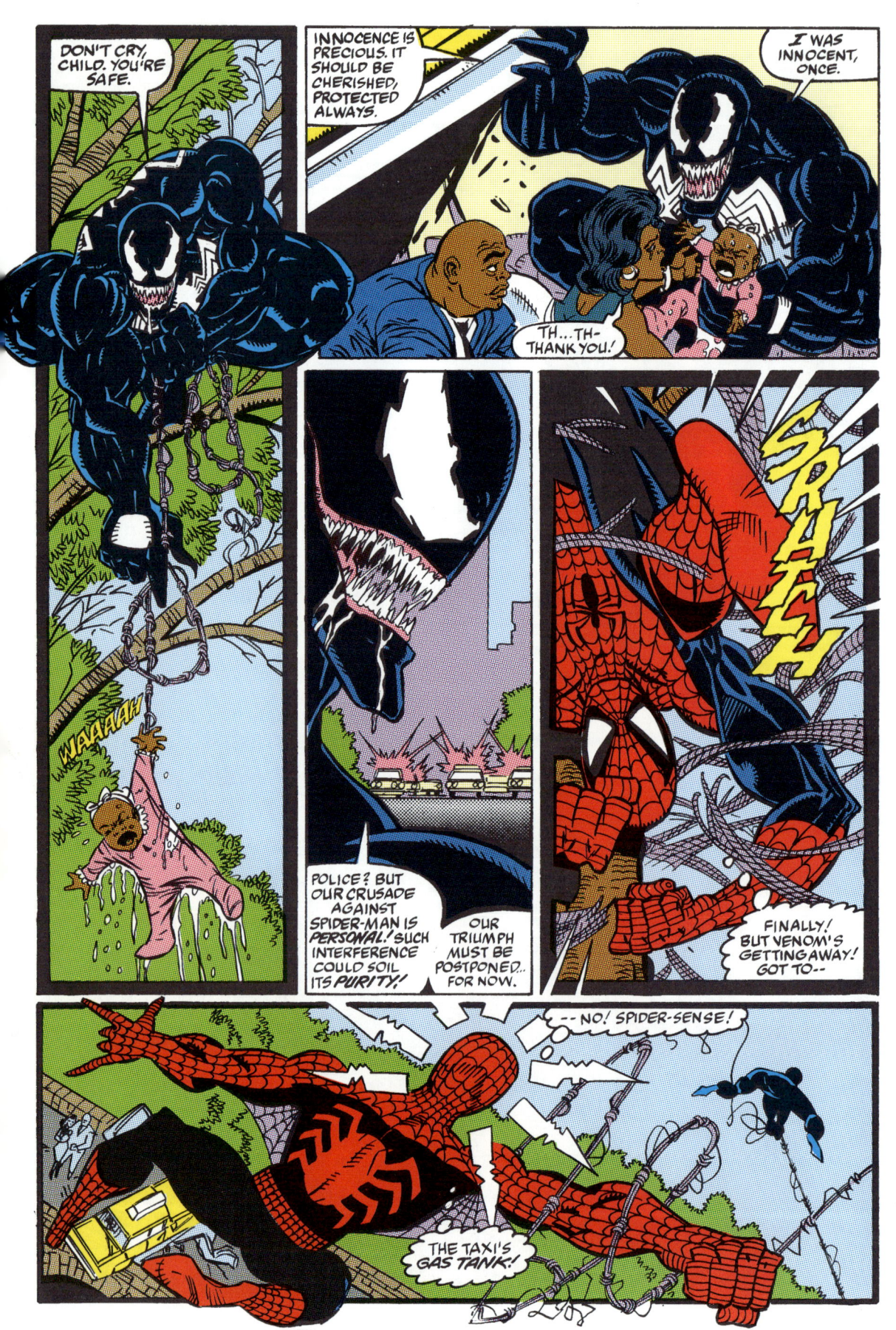

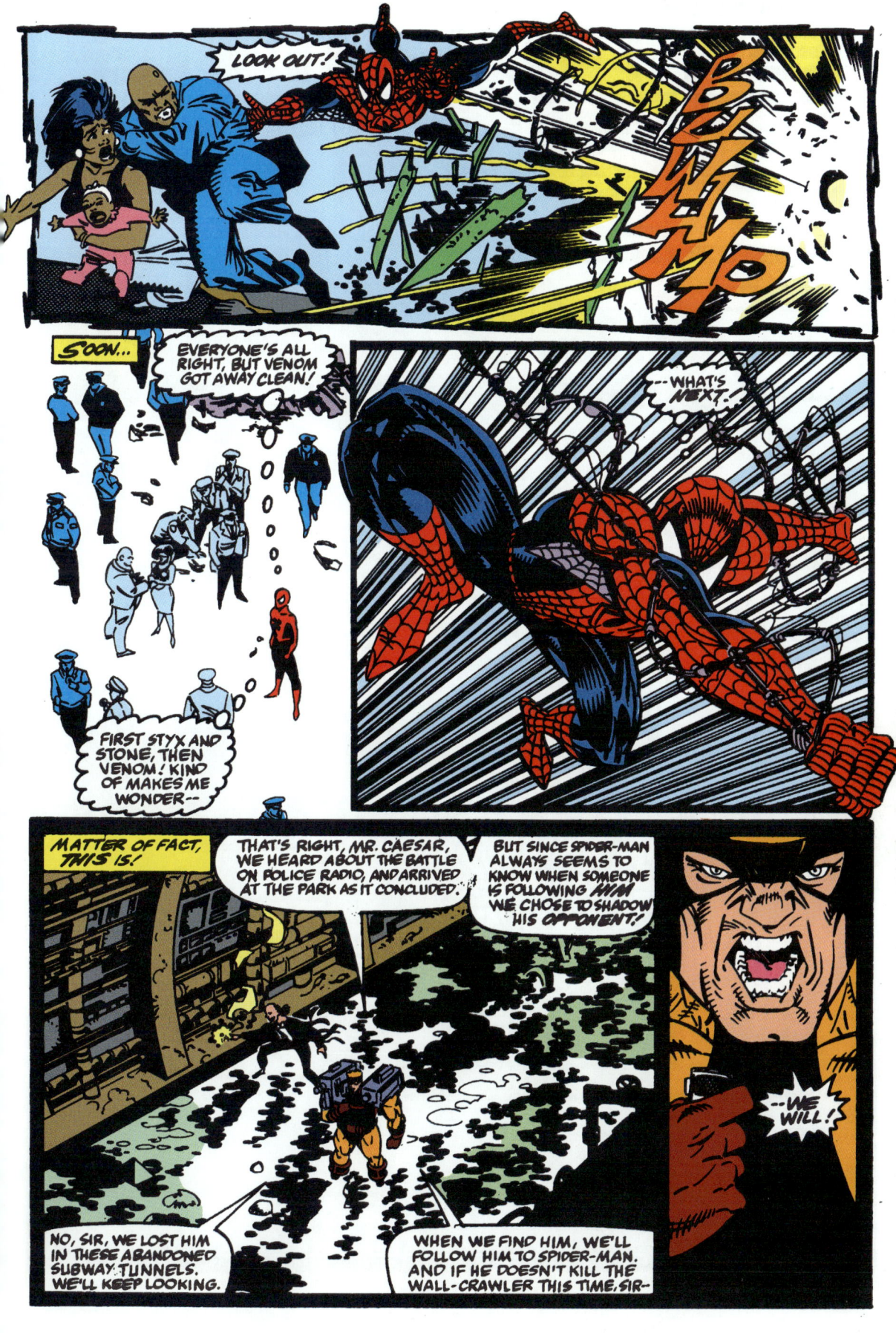

CHAPTER TWO

STALKING FEAR!

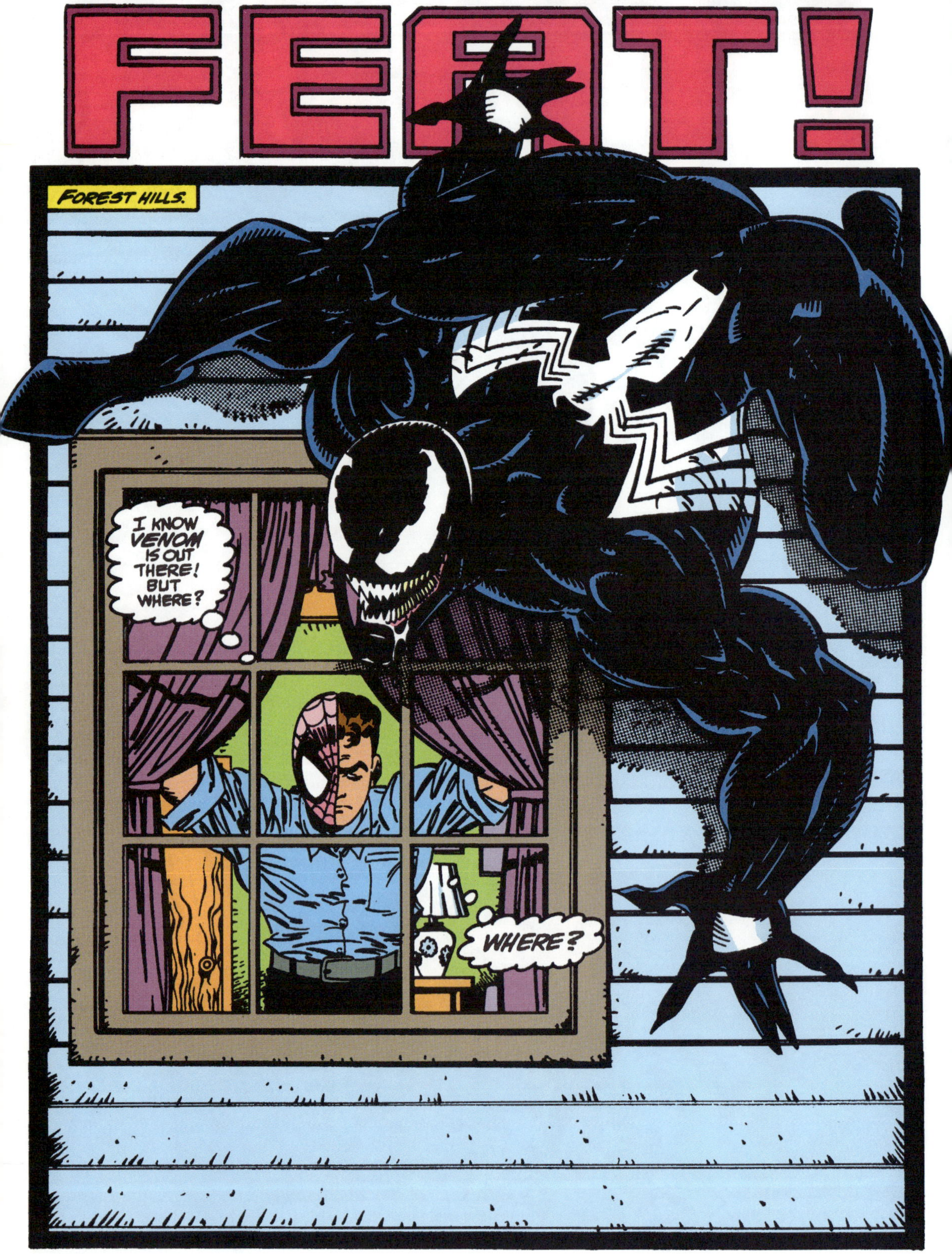

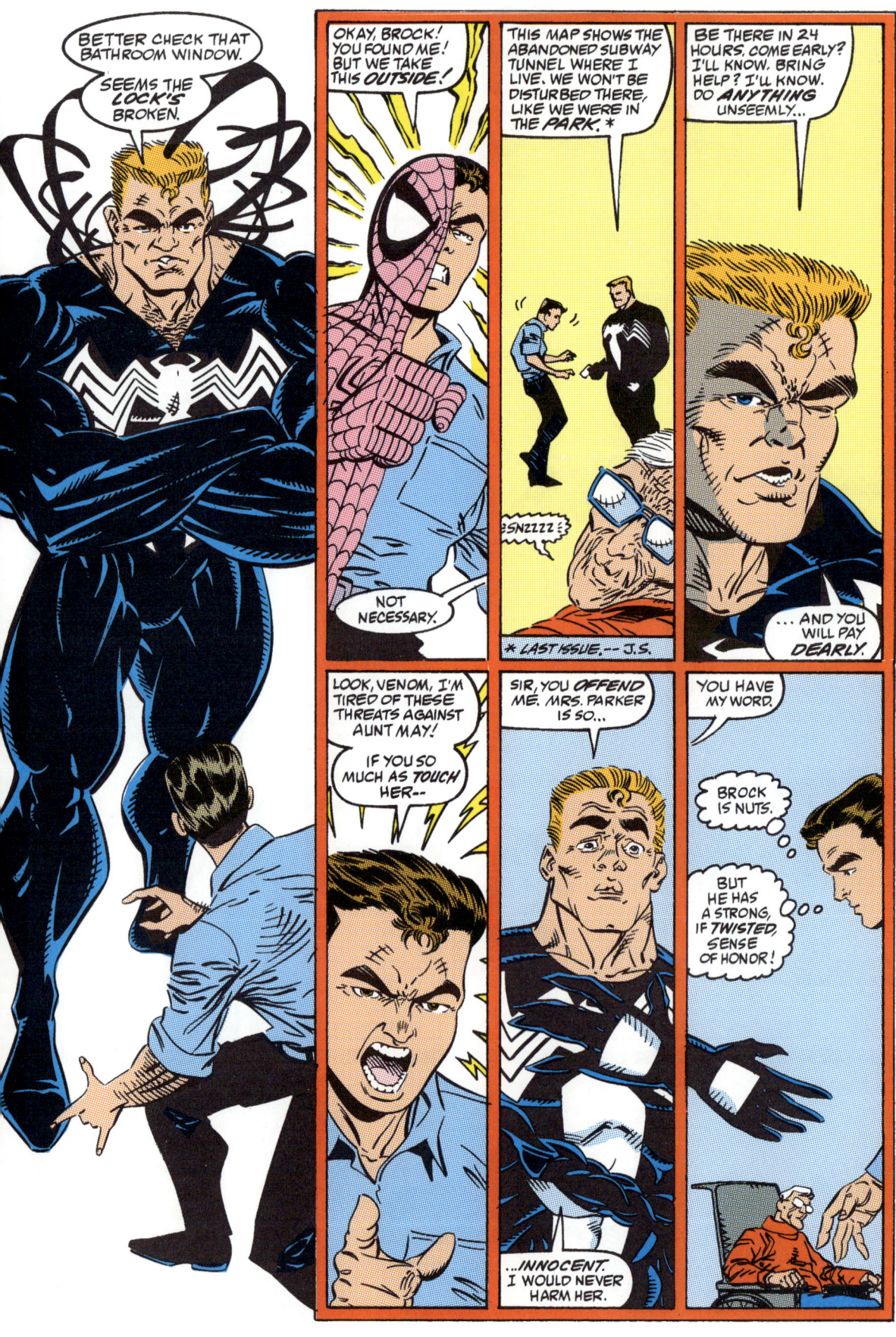

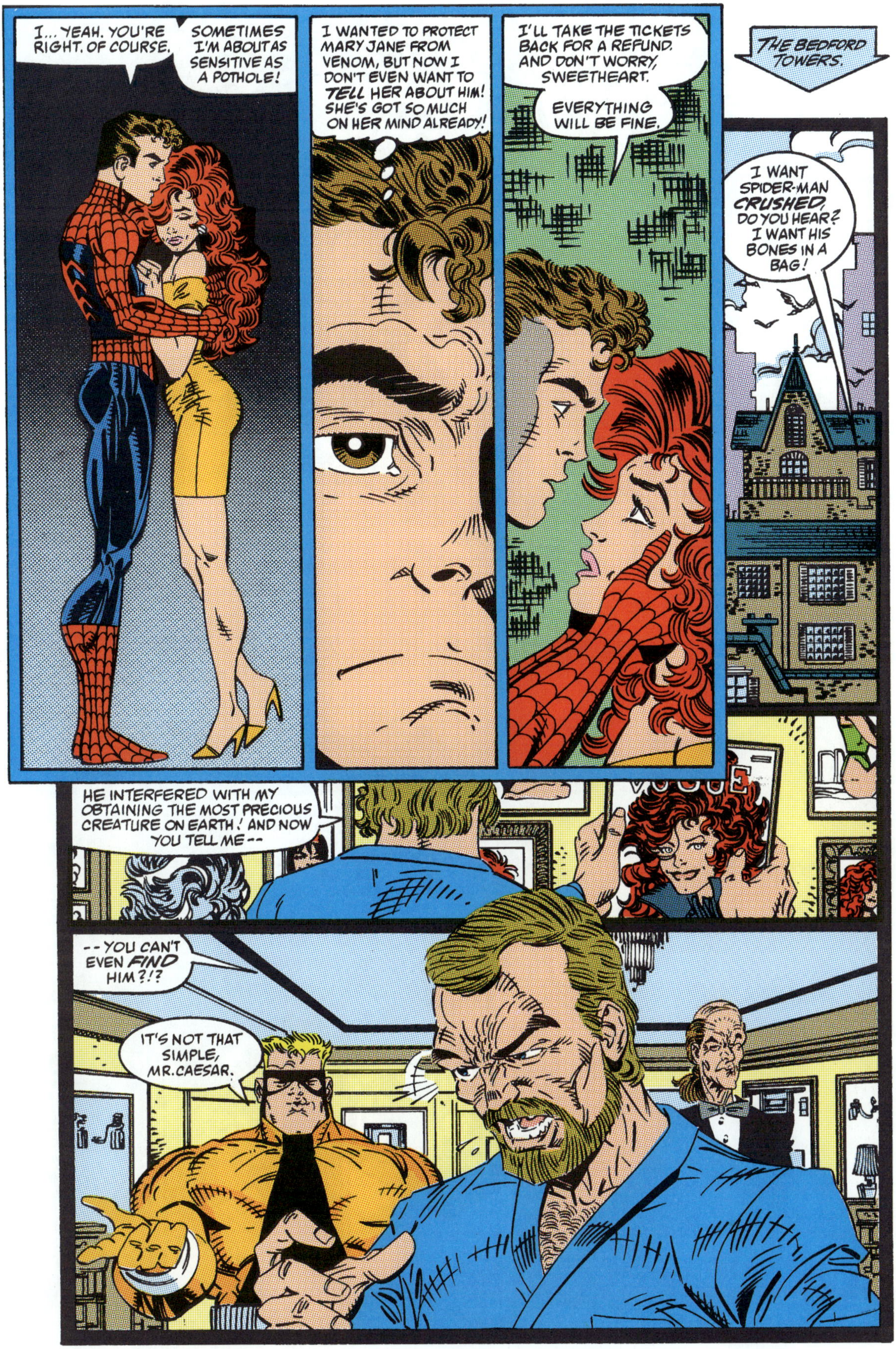
I... YEAH. YOU'RE RIGHT, OF COURSE.
SOMETIMES I'M ABOUT AS SENSITIVE AS A POTHOLE!
I WANTED TO PROTECT MARY JANE FROM VENOM, BUT NOW I DON'T EVEN WANT TO TELL HER ABOUT HIM! SHE'S GOT SO MUCH ON HER MIND ALREADY!
I'LL TAKE THE TICKETS BACK FOR A REFUND. AND DON'T WORRY, SWEETHEART.
EVERYTHING WILL BE FINE.
THE BEDFORD TOWERS.
I WANT SPIDER-MAN CRUSHED, DO YOU HEAR? I WANT HIS BONES IN A BAG!
HE INTERFERED WITH MY OBTAINING THE MOST PRECIOUS CREATURE ON EARTH! AND NOW YOU TELL ME--
VOGUE
--YOU CAN'T EVEN FIND HIM?!?
IT'S NOT THAT SIMPLE, MR. CAESAR.

WE REACHED CENTRAL PARK JUST AS THE FIGHT BETWEEN SPIDER-MAN AND VENOM WAS ENDING. FROM EXPERIENCE, WE KNEW THAT FOLLOWING *SPIDER-MAN* WOULD BE FUTILE-- HE ALWAYS SEEMS TO KNOW WHEN SOMEONE'S TAILING HIM.

SO WE CHOSE TO SHADOW *VENOM* INSTEAD, THINKING THAT HIS APPARENT HATRED FOR THE WEBSLINGER WOULD EVENTUALLY BRING THE TWO *TOGETHER* AGAIN.

BUT WE LOST HIM IN A MAZE OF ABANDONED SUBWAY TUNNELS. WE SUSPECT HE HAS OTHER MODES OF EGRESS, PERHAPS EVEN SOME WAY TO *DISGUISE* HIMSELF. BUT--

Panel 1:
-- eh? STYX! DON'T--!
MMMMMM...!
CAN'T YOU MAKE HIM STOP THAT?
SSSSS

Panel 2:
WAIT WITH THE TURBO-HOPPER IN THE ALLEY! KILL SOME COCKROACHES!
BUT ⸘SNIFF⸮ THEY'RE SO SMALL!
NORMALLY, MR. STONE, I RESPECT MY OPERATIVES' PRIVACY, BUT--

Panel 3:
-- WHAT THE BLAZES IS HE?!

Panel 4:
A VICTIM, SIR. SOME TIME BACK, A LEGITIMATE MEDICAL RESEARCH FIRM WAS HIRING HOMELESS PEOPLE TO PARTICIPATE IN EXPERIMENTS FOR NEW PHARMACEUTICALS. PAY WAS GOOD; DANGER WAS MINIMAL.

BUT ONE SCIENTIST PURSUED HIS OWN UNAUTHORIZED PROJECT, EXPLORING A THEORY THAT THE BODY COULD DEVELOP IMMUNITY TO CANCER BY CONTROLLED EXPOSURE, SIMILAR TO THE WAY IT CAN COME TO TOLERATE SNAKE POISON. TO THAT END, AN ITINERANT NAMED JACOB EICHORN WAS INJECTED WITH A MUTATED CANCER COMPOUND BUT IN ADDITION TO DEVELOPING IMMUNITY--

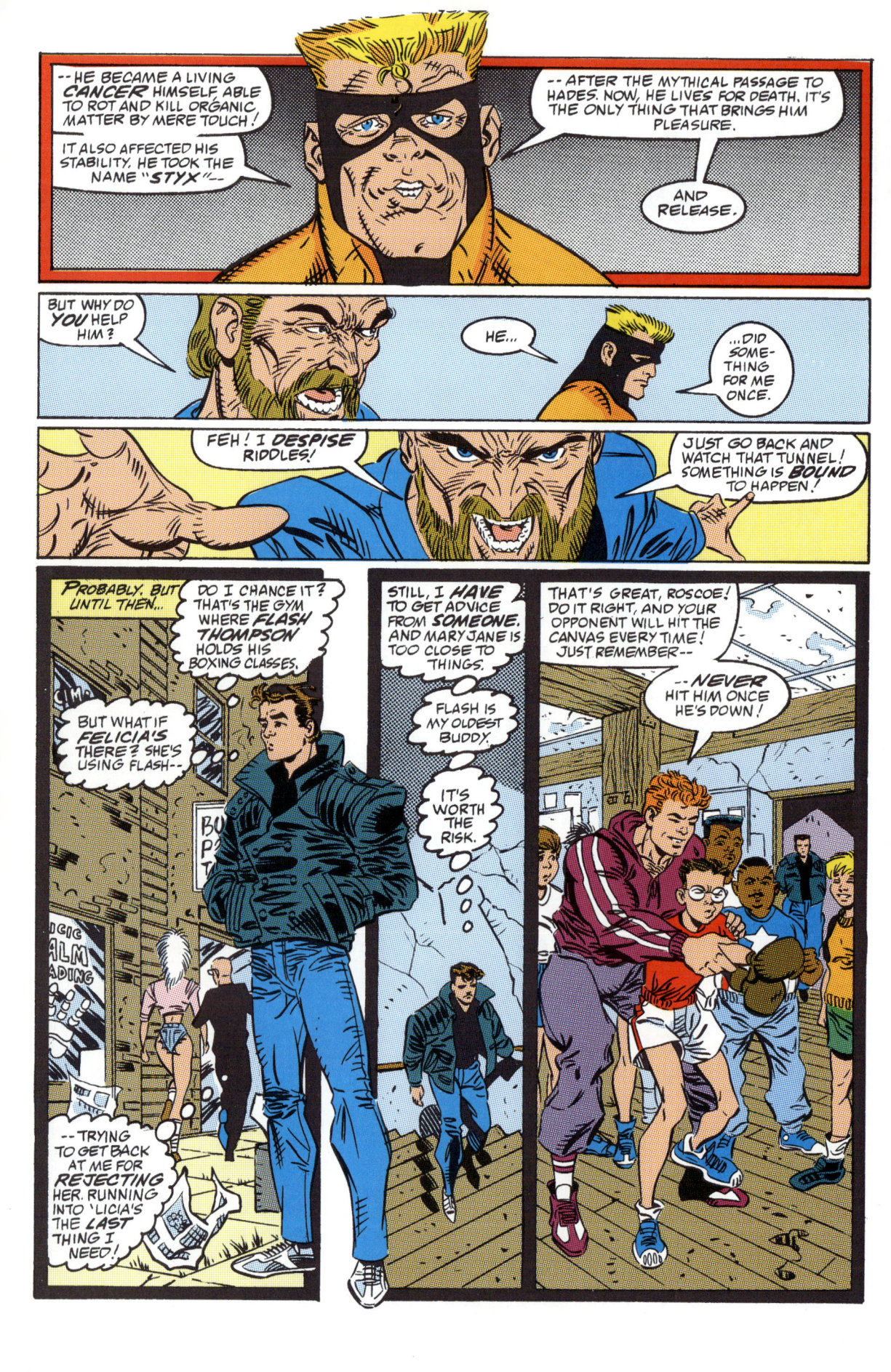

-- HE BECAME A LIVING *CANCER* HIMSELF, ABLE TO ROT AND KILL ORGANIC MATTER BY MERE TOUCH!

IT ALSO AFFECTED HIS STABILITY. HE TOOK THE NAME *"STYX"*--

-- AFTER THE MYTHICAL PASSAGE TO HADES. NOW, HE LIVES FOR DEATH. IT'S THE ONLY THING THAT BRINGS HIM PLEASURE.

AND RELEASE.

BUT WHY DO *YOU* HELP HIM?

HE...

...DID SOMETHING FOR ME ONCE.

FEH! I *DESPISE* RIDDLES!

JUST GO BACK AND WATCH THAT TUNNEL! SOMETHING IS *BOUND* TO HAPPEN!

Probably. But until then...

DO I CHANCE IT? THAT'S THE GYM WHERE *FLASH THOMPSON* HOLDS HIS BOXING CLASSES.

BUT WHAT IF *FELICIA'S* THERE? SHE'S USING FLASH--

STILL, I *HAVE* TO GET ADVICE FROM *SOMEONE*. AND MARY JANE IS TOO CLOSE TO THINGS.

FLASH IS MY OLDEST BUDDY.

IT'S WORTH THE RISK.

THAT'S GREAT, ROSCOE! DO IT RIGHT, AND YOUR OPPONENT WILL HIT THE CANVAS EVERY TIME! JUST REMEMBER--

--*NEVER* HIT HIM ONCE HE'S DOWN!

--TRYING TO GET BACK AT ME FOR *REJECTING* HER. RUNNING INTO 'LICIA'S THE *LAST* THING I NEED!

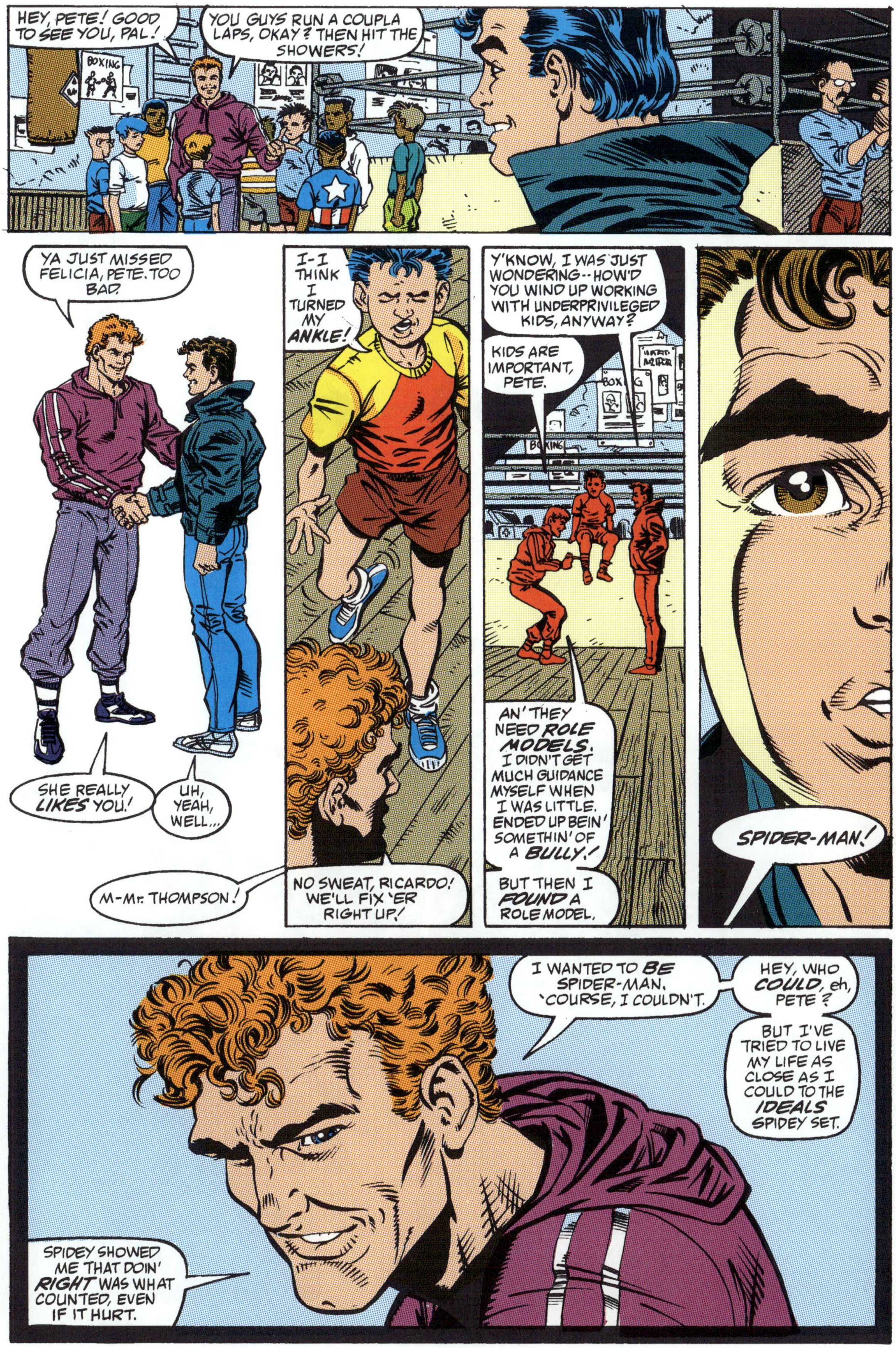

HEY, PETE! GOOD TO SEE YOU, PAL!
YOU GUYS RUN A COUPLA LAPS, OKAY? THEN HIT THE SHOWERS!
BOXING
YA JUST MISSED FELICIA, PETE. TOO BAD.
SHE REALLY LIKES YOU!
UH, YEAH, WELL...
I-I THINK I TURNED MY ANKLE!
M-Mr. THOMPSON!
NO SWEAT, RICARDO! WE'LL FIX 'ER RIGHT UP!
Y'KNOW, I WAS JUST WONDERING--HOW'D YOU WIND UP WORKING WITH UNDERPRIVILEGED KIDS, ANYWAY?
KIDS ARE IMPORTANT, PETE.
AN' THEY NEED ROLE MODELS. I DIDN'T GET MUCH GUIDANCE MYSELF WHEN I WAS LITTLE. ENDED UP BEIN' SOMETHIN' OF A BULLY!
BUT THEN I FOUND A ROLE MODEL.
SPIDER-MAN!
I WANTED TO BE SPIDER-MAN. 'COURSE, I COULDN'T.
HEY, WHO COULD, eh, PETE?
BUT I'VE TRIED TO LIVE MY LIFE AS CLOSE AS I COULD TO THE IDEALS SPIDEY SET.
SPIDEY SHOWED ME THAT DOIN' RIGHT WAS WHAT COUNTED, EVEN IF IT HURT.

SOMETIMES IT ISN'T EASY. PROBLEMS SEEM BIGGER'N LIFE.
BUT I ALWAYS KEEP TRYIN'.
'CAUSE I KNOW SPIDEY WOULDN'T GIVE UP JUST BECAUSE THE GOIN' GOT TOUGH!
YOU WALK THAT ON OUT, RICKY. IT'LL BE FINE TOMORROW.
NOW, PAL, WHAT CAN I DO FOR YOU?
I THINK YOU'VE ALREADY DONE IT.
PAL!
BOXIN
TONITE!
FIGHT
BATTLE OF THE CENTURY
BOXING!
THE WAR!
LIEFELD VS McFARLANE
CENTRAL PARK, EVENING.
YOU'RE KILLING OUR COVER!
I'M BORED.
FSSS
CUT IT OUT, STYX!

"THAT CAN'T BE HELPED! JUST KEEP YOUR--"

"--GLOVES ON?"

"NEVER MIND."

"BOREDOM'S OVER!"

GOT TO BE CAREFUL!

REAL CAREFUL!

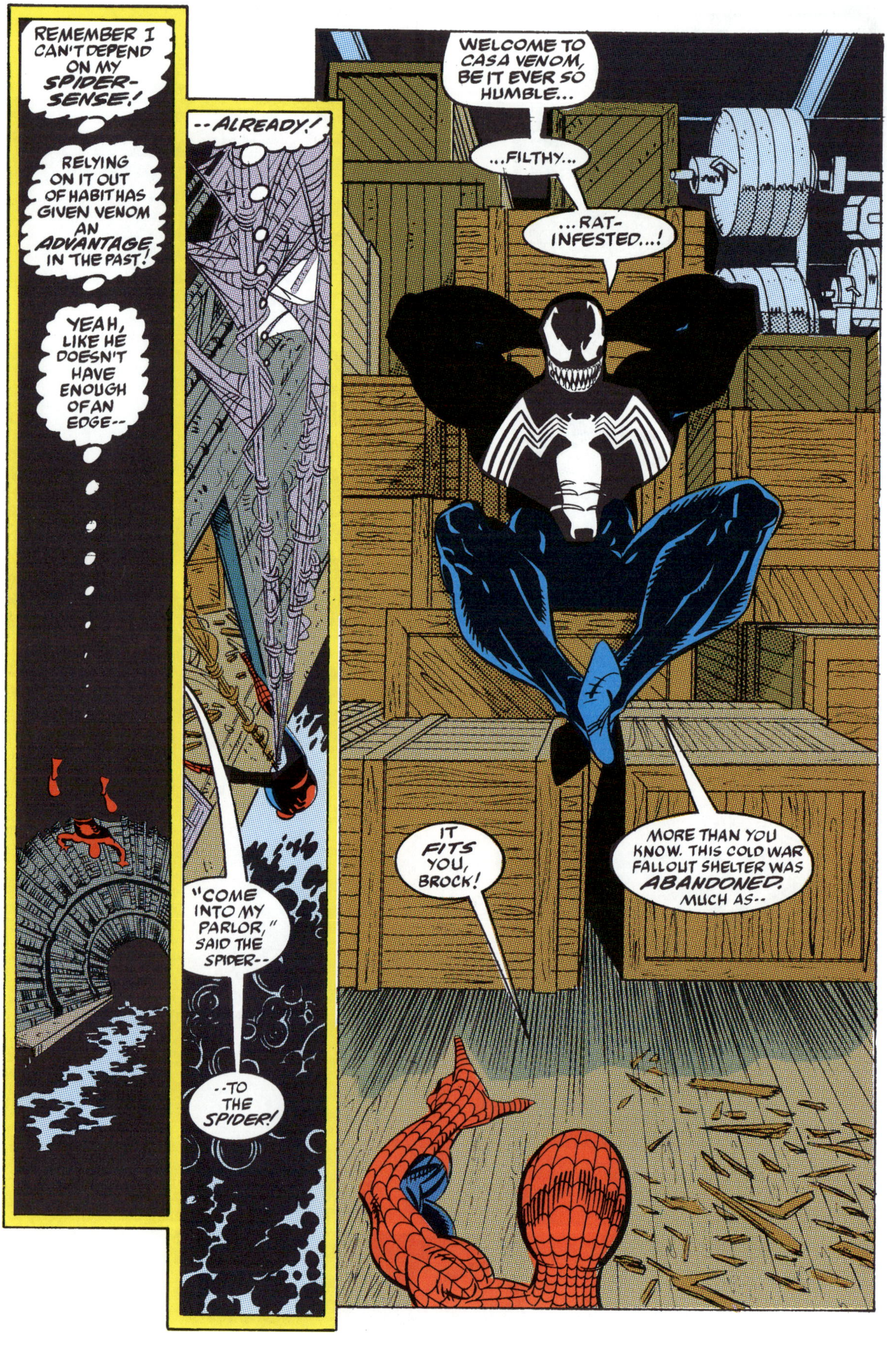
REMEMBER I CAN'T DEPEND ON MY SPIDER-SENSE!
RELYING ON IT OUT OF HABIT HAS GIVEN VENOM AN ADVANTAGE IN THE PAST!
YEAH, LIKE HE DOESN'T HAVE ENOUGH OF AN EDGE--
--ALREADY!
"COME INTO MY PARLOR," SAID THE SPIDER--
--TO THE SPIDER!
WELCOME TO CASA VENOM, BE IT EVER SO HUMBLE...
...FILTHY...
...RAT-INFESTED...!
IT FITS YOU, BROCK!
MORE THAN YOU KNOW. THIS COLD WAR FALLOUT SHELTER WAS ABANDONED. MUCH AS--

--WE WERE! I, WHEN MY JOURNALISTIC CAREER WAS DESTROYED! AND MY OTHER-WORLDLY COMRADE--
--WHEN IT WAS SPURNED BY THE HUMAN IT HAD ORIGINALLY JOINED!
THE SOURCE OF PAIN IN BOTH INSTANCES BEING--
...YOU!
SOMETHING'S WRONG! HE'S TALKING INSTEAD OF ATTACKING! GOT TO HAVE SOMETHING UP HIS--
--SLEEVE? SENT SOME OF THE ALIEN'S SUBSTANCE ALONG THE FLOOR, HIDING IT IN THE SHADOWS! TRIED TO AMBUSH ME--
--LIKE HE DID ON THAT LONG ISLAND BEACH!*
*IN ISSUE #317. --J.S.

BUT A WEBLINE, JUDICIOUSLY APPLIED TO THOSE *BARBELLS!*

KRMBLLNK

--NYYAAGGH!

THWIPP

MISSED ME! NYAH, NYAH--

WE DON'T WANT TO PLAY ANYMORE.

NO?

NOPE.

WE WANT TO EAT YOUR BRAIN!
SPIDER-SENSE! VENOM ?!? NO!
COMING FROM--
SHHKAKUNK
--BEHIND!

WHA--? AW, NO! NOT--
HNGF
"--THEM!"
SHALL I REMOVE MY GLOVES, Mr. STONE?
NOW'S THE TIME, Mr. STYX!
NEW RULES?
PERHAPS WE WILL PLAY A LITTLE LONGER!
YAAAAGH!
SREE REEEEEEE
SONIC BEAM WAS PAINFUL WHEN IT WAS USED AGAINST ME!
BUT IT COULD HAVE DEADLY EFFECTS ON THE SYMBIOTE!

BLAST IT ALL! BENEATH THAT COSTUME, EDDIE BROCK IS JUST A SCREWED-UP HUMAN BEING!
I CAN'T STAND AROUND AND WATCH HIM--
--DIE?
WHEW! AT LEAST MY SPIDER-SENSE STILL WORKS ON THESE GUYS! GOT TO WATCH THOSE HANDS!
MAKE SURE THEY DON'T EVEN GRAZE MY-- EH? THE FINGERS!
G-GROWING LONGER?!
THIS IS GETTING COMPLICATED!
PHOOF
K-KOFF
GAS PODS SLOWING THE WEBSLINGER DOWN! FINISH HIM OFF, STYX!
I'LL KEEP VENOM BUSY!

I-IT WAS TOUGH AVOIDING THESE GAS PELLETS ≷CHOKE≶ IN THE OPEN AIR!
H-HOW CAN I STAY AWAY FROM THEM *HERE*?
HEAT RAY?
"NOVA BEAM."
OOOOO, SPIFFY NAME!
I THINK WE'LL CALL THIS BROKEN WATER PIPE "*RODNEY*"!
PLACE LOOKS LIKE IT WAS A FALLOUT SHELTER! SUPPLIES PROBABLY DATE BACK TO THE *COLD WAR*! BUT THEY'RE STILL SOLID ENOUGH TO--
"--LORD! OATS TURNING BLACK! RUNNING LIKE *SYRUP*! TH-THIS GUY EVEN ROTS 40-YEAR-OLD GRAIN!"

MEANWHILE...
CASH
STROBE BURST SHOULD BLIND HIM! THEN--
--HNH? Y-YOUR EYES! THEY'RE GONE!
UH-UH.
JUST HIDING!
PEEKABOO!
?
CH-CH-CH CH CHK
OUCH.
PLIP
PLIP
PLIP

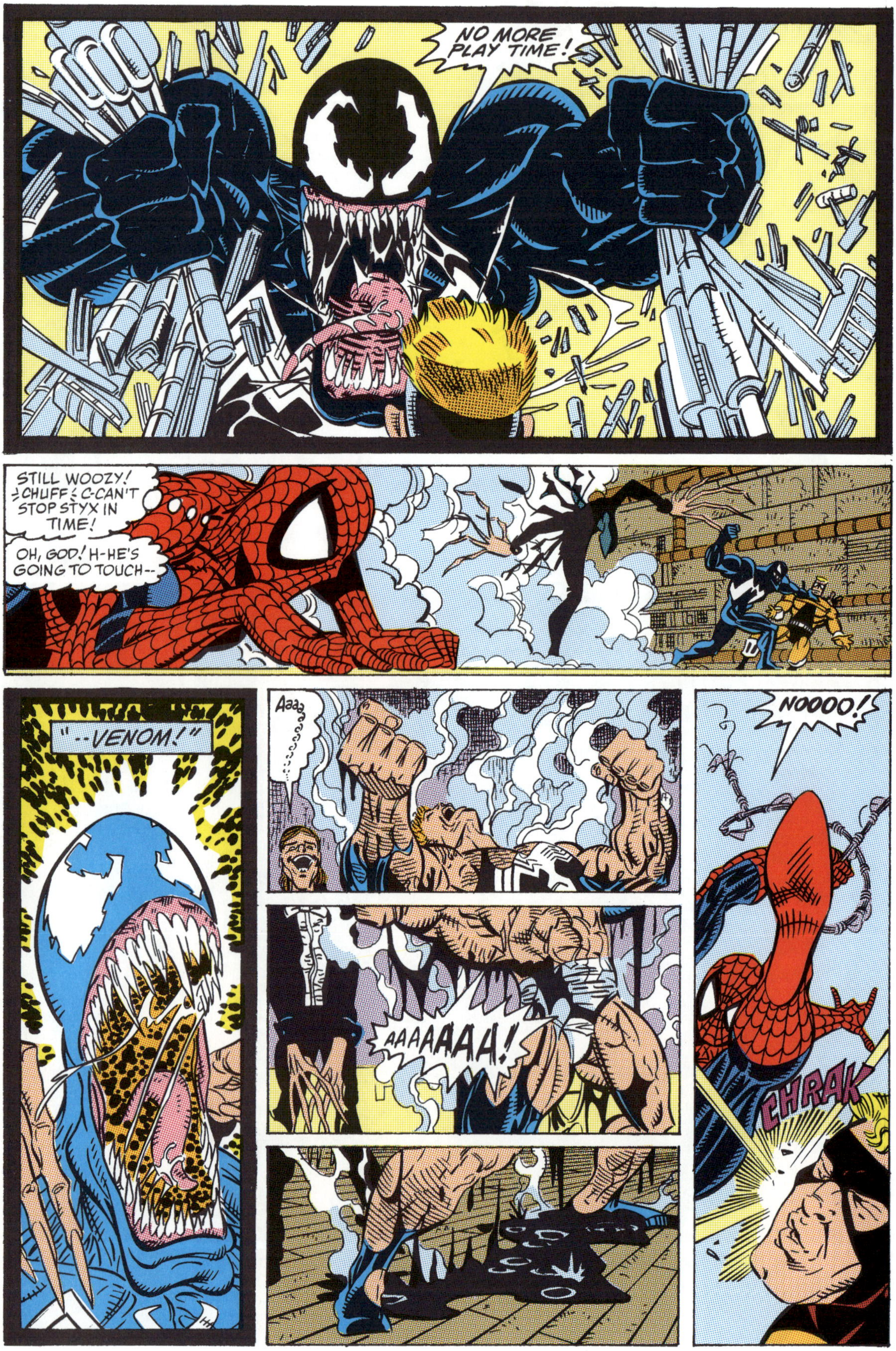
NO MORE PLAY TIME!
STILL WOOZY! *CHUFF* C-CAN'T STOP STYX IN TIME!
OH, GOD! H-HE'S GOING TO TOUCH--
"--VENOM!"
Aaaa
AAAAAAA!
NOOOO!
CHRAK

MANIAC'S IN ECSTASY! NOT EVEN TRYING TO ESCAPE!
BUT WHAT ABOUT--
--VENOM?
WE... SNIFF
...W-WE'RE... SNUFFLE...
..DEAD!
SOMETIME LATER...
THEY'RE TAKING BROCK TO RYKER'S ISLAND--NO NEED FOR THE VAULT ANYMORE.
WHATEVER IT IS STYX DISHES OUT, THE SYMBIOTE TOOK ALL OF IT! GAVE ITS LIFE FOR EDDIE'S!
I'LL PUT THE REMAINS WHERE THEY'LL BE SAFE.
SHOULD BE HAPPY. BUT EVEN WITH THE EVIDENCE HERE IN MY HANDS, IT'S HARD TO BELIEVE THAT AT LAST, THE MENACE OF VENOM...
...IS OVER!

Convinced the alien costume was no longer a threat, Spider-Man left, carelessly thinking it would never trouble him again; Styx and Stone were led away in chains.

Eddie Brock was incarcerated in Ryker's Island Prison, where he was placed with the general population. As far as Eddie was concerned, his symbiotic partner was dead, and he now had one more reason to hate Spider-Man.

Brock's cellmate was a serial killer named Cletus Kasady. Now, we join them in their cell...

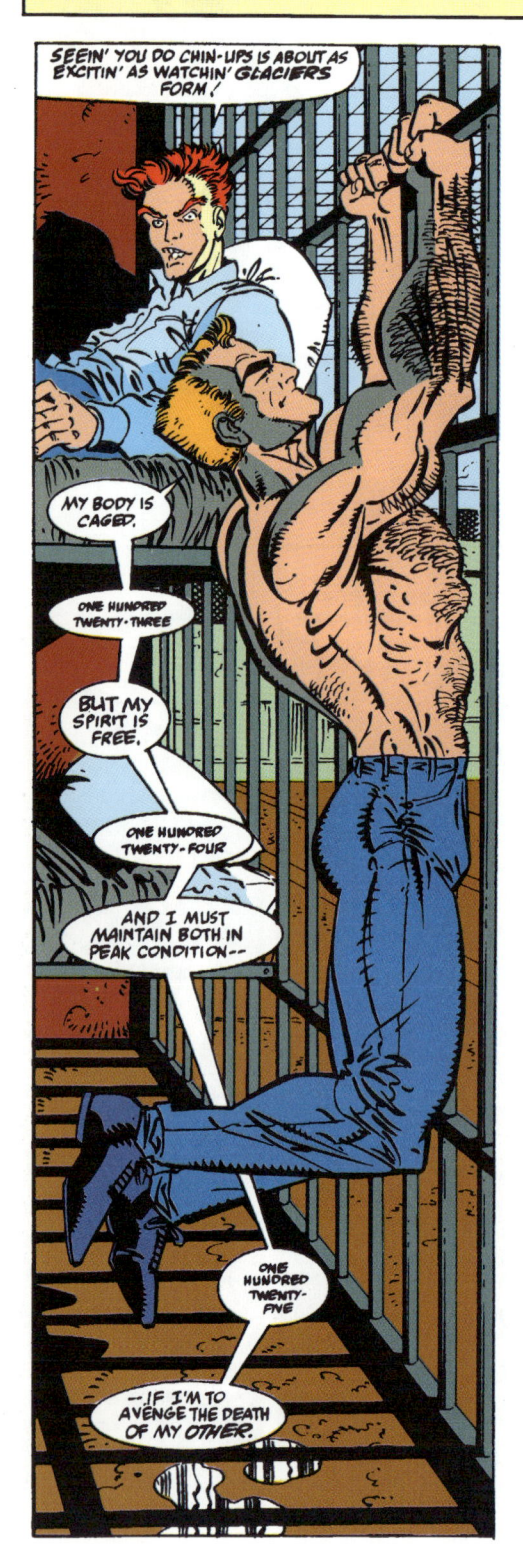

SEEIN' YOU DO CHIN-UPS IS ABOUT AS EXCITIN' AS WATCHIN' GLACIERS FORM!

MY BODY IS CAGED.

ONE HUNDRED TWENTY-THREE

BUT MY SPIRIT IS FREE.

ONE HUNDRED TWENTY-FOUR

AND I MUST MAINTAIN BOTH IN PEAK CONDITION--

ONE HUNDRED TWENTY-FIVE

--IF I'M TO AVENGE THE DEATH OF MY *OTHER*.

FORGET THAT *VENOM* SPOOK! ALL YA NEED IS *WILL*!

THE COURAGE TO *DO* THINGS OTHER FOLKS ARE *SCARED* TO!

LIKE *SLAUGHTERING* INNOCENT FAMILIES, CLETUS? ≽sigh≼

SOMETIMES I WISH I DIDN'T HAVE TO LIVE WITH A FOUL *SERIAL KILLER* LIKE YOU.

KEEP GRIPIN', PAL, AN' YA WON'T BE!

eep!

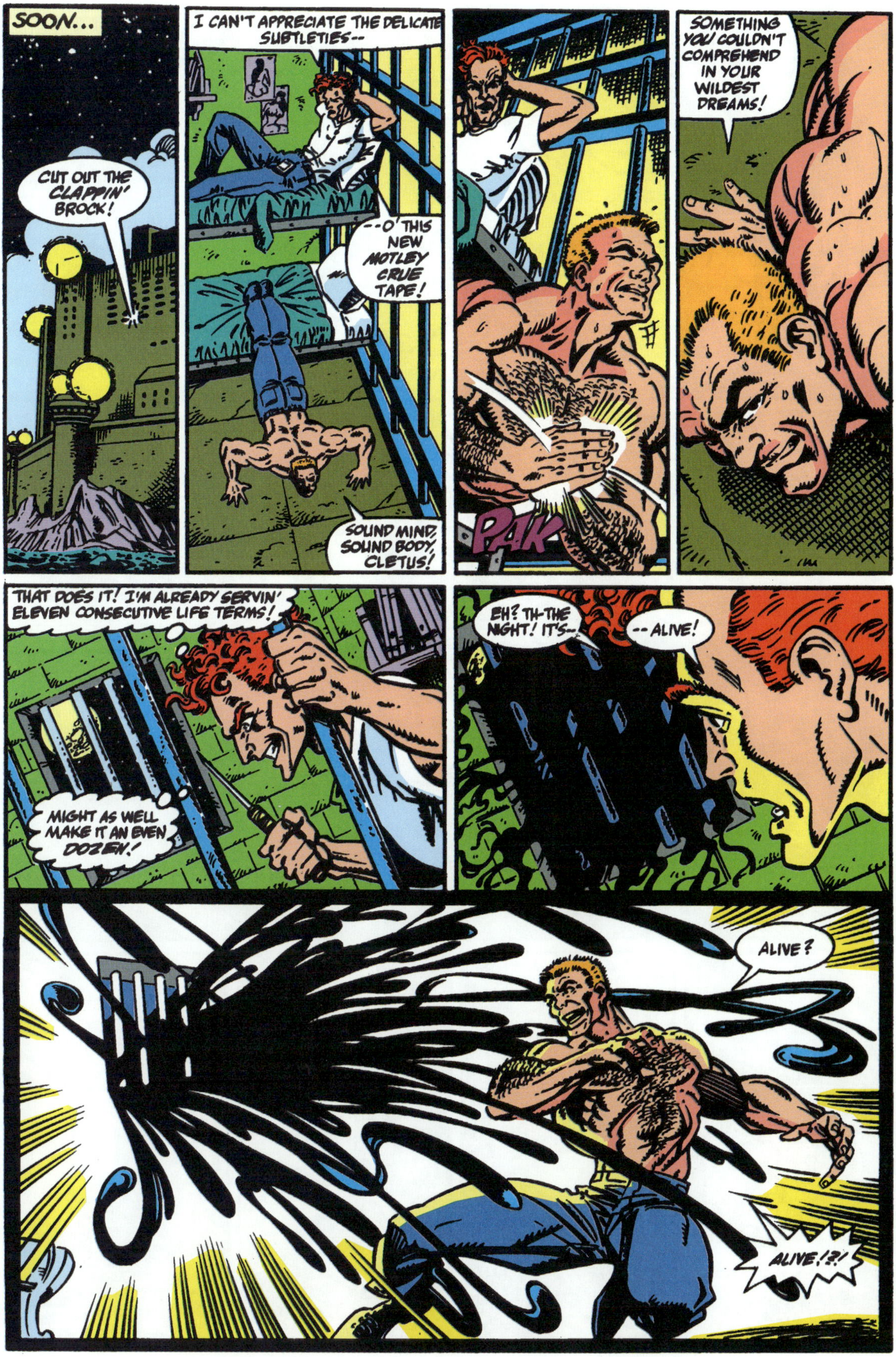
SOON...
CUT OUT THE CLAPPIN' BROCK!
I CAN'T APPRECIATE THE DELICATE SUBTLETIES--
--O' THIS NEW MOTLEY CRUE TAPE!
SOUND MIND, SOUND BODY, CLETUS!
PAK
SOMETHING YOU COULDN'T COMPREHEND IN YOUR WILDEST DREAMS!
THAT DOES IT! I'M ALREADY SERVIN' ELEVEN CONSECUTIVE LIFE TERMS!
MIGHT AS WELL MAKE IT AN EVEN DOZEN!
EH? TH-THE NIGHT! IT'S--
--ALIVE!
ALIVE?
ALIVE!?!

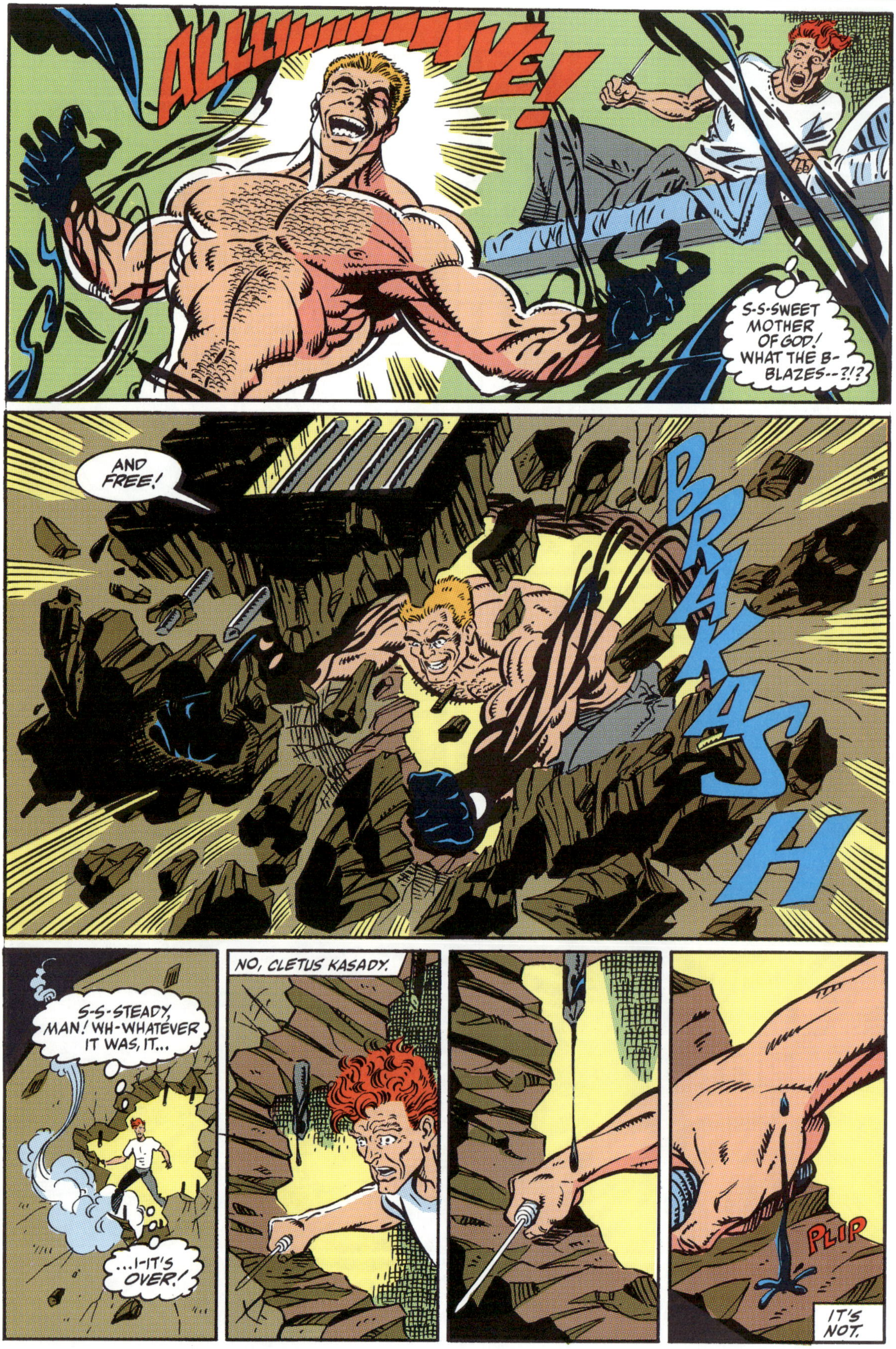
ALLIIIIIIIIIVE!
S-S-SWEET MOTHER OF GOD! WHAT THE B-BLAZES--?!?
AND FREE!
BRAKASH
S-S-STEADY, MAN! WH-WHATEVER IT WAS, IT...
...I-IT'S OVER!
NO, CLETUS KASADY.
PLIP
IT'S NOT.

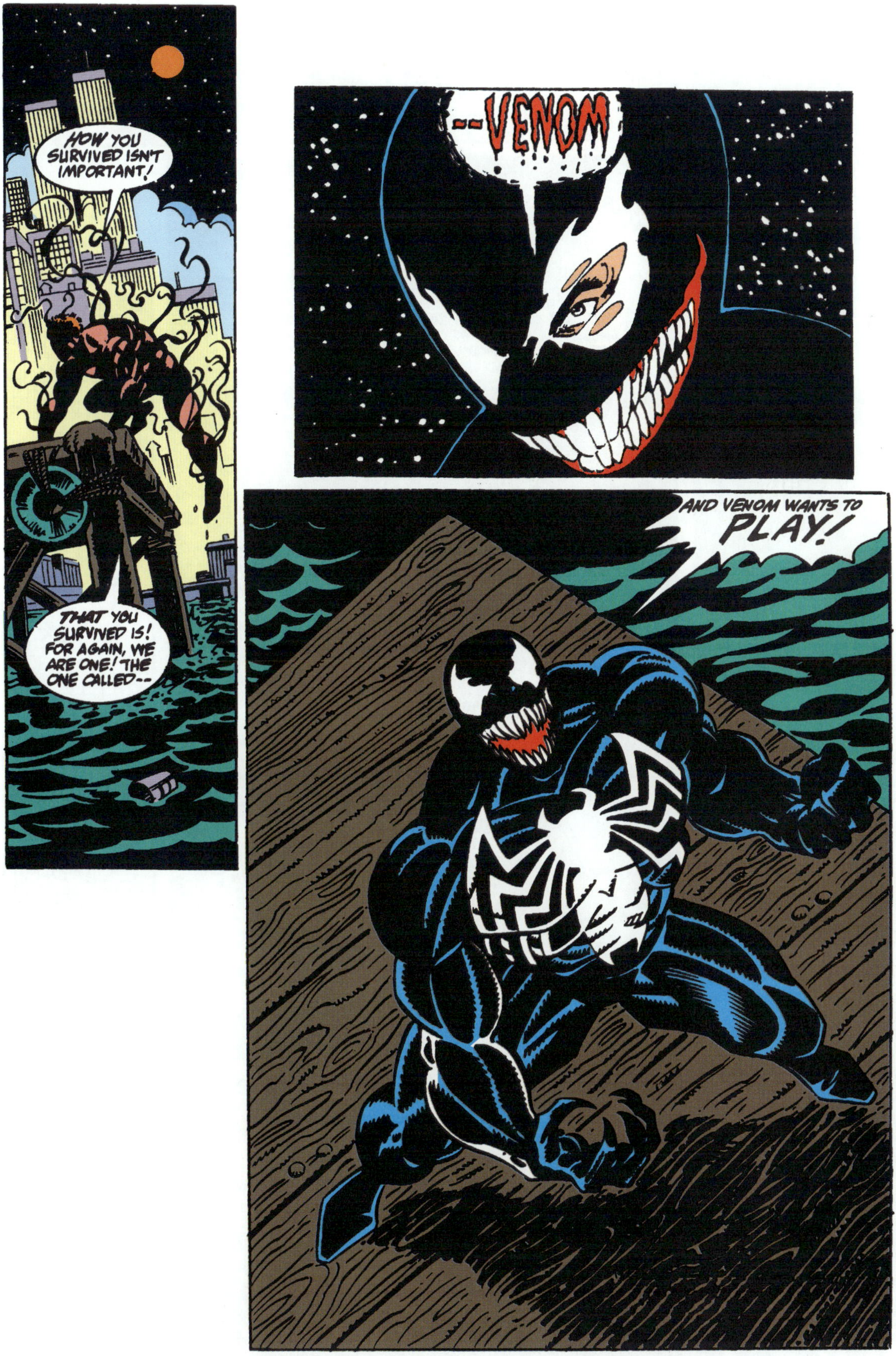
HOW YOU SURVIVED ISN'T IMPORTANT!
THAT YOU SURVIVED IS! FOR AGAIN, WE ARE ONE! THE ONE CALLED--
--VENOM
AND VENOM WANTS TO PLAY!

CHAPTER THREE

They say New York never sleeps.

Phooey.

On a Sunday night, the city practically snores!

Even the offices of the usually-bustling Daily Globe seem deserted.

Which is exactly how Sly Fenster likes it.

With only a skeleton crew on duty, there's less chance of being disturbed.

Or caught.

You see, Sly's been tapping other reporters' databases, pulling confidential files, private info and not-for-print revelations by actors, politicians and the like.

The cash paid by supermarket tabloids for these scoops makes life easier, though it doesn't make a lot of friends.

But, hey-- who needs friends? Right, Sly?

Especially--

--with enemies like this?!

GASP

ELLIPTICAL PURSUIT!

"YOU KNOW, SLY... I NEVER *DID* LIKE YOU!"

NO! P-P- PLEASE--!
THE FOURTH ESTATE IS A NOBLE INSTITUTION! ONE I REVERED WHEN I WAS WITH THE GLOBE!
I ALWAYS SUSPECTED YOU DIDN'T SHARE THAT REVERENCE, SLY!
BUT RIGHT NOW, WE HAVE MORE IMPORTANT MATTERS TO TEND TO!
PLIP
GLMF
WHEN I WAS IN PRISON, I READ OF EXPERIMENTS THAT MIGHT AID OUR QUEST FOR JUSTICE!
CHGK
BUT THERE ARE DETAILS WE MUST HAVE IN ORDER TO--
RLNK
--AH. THIS IS PRECISELY WHAT WE NEED!
NOW, SLY, FOR YOUR--
--PUNISHMENT? OH, DEAR. HE APPEARS TO HAVE SUFFOCATED.
WE'RE SO SORRY.
YOU WERE A WORM, SLY, BUT THERE'S NO GLORY IN YOUR PASSING.
NO, NOT LIKE THERE WILL BE...
...WHEN WE KILL SPIDER-MAN!

GRAND CENTRAL STATION: WHERE A SOMEWHAT GENTLER CONFLICT IS PLAYED OUT...
TRY TO UNDERSTAND, MARY JANE -- IT'S FOR THE BEST!
SENDING ME TO VISIT MY SISTER, WHEN YOU COULD BE KILLED AT ANY MINUTE?
THAT'S NOT THE BEST OF ANYTHING!
IT IS! IT'S THAT BABE ON TV!
I'LL BET SHE WANTS ME...!
GRAND CENTRAL TERMINAL
LOOK, WHEN EDDIE BROCK BROKE OUT OF PRISON, I CALLED THE FANTASTIC FOUR!
THEY SAID THE "DEAD" ALIEN COSTUME HAD ESCAPED, TOO! THAT MEANS VENOM IS BACK!
AND HE'LL BE COMING AFTER ME, MJ.
AFTER SPIDER-MAN!
BUT, I THOUGHT WE WERE PARTNERS...!

"WE *ARE!* BUT EVEN WITH VENOM'S TWISTED SENSE OF ETHICS, HOW HE SAYS HE WON'T HARM "INNOCENTS"--

AND I CAN'T WATCH MY *BACK* IF I'M WATCHING OUT FOR *YOU!*

PLEASE, SWEETHEART?

OH... ALL RIGHT.

BUT I HATE IT.

SO DO I.

"HOW TO CREATE A HAPPY MARRIAGE," BY PETER PARKER. CHAPTER ONE:

DON'T DO THIS!

--HE'S STILL A *MADMAN!* HE MIGHT USE YOU TO GET AT *ME!*

STILL, A BIT LATER, IN SOHO...

HNH? OH, GREAT. GOT LOST IN THOUGHT.

WALKED HOME OUT OF HABIT!

CAN'T STAY HERE! IT'S THE FIRST PLACE VENOM WOULD--

A PESO FOR YOUR THOUGHTS, KIMO SABE!

HEY, FLASH! 'LO, FELICIA. WHAT'S UP?

NOT THE *TEMPERATURE,* BUDDY! WE'RE GOIN' ICE SKATIN'! HOW 'BOUT COMIN' ALONG?

"CAN'T PUT *FRIENDS* IN DANGER!

GEE, GUYS, I'M AFRAID I HAVE TO DO SOME WORK OVER AT THE UNIVERSITY!"

"ARE YOU *SURE* I CAN'T HELP?"

"THANKS, 'LICIA, BUT THIS IS SOMETHING *I* HAVE TO HANDLE."

SHE KNOWS.

FELICIA WAS THE BLACK CAT. SHE UNDERSTANDS VENOM.

BUT EVEN BEFORE SHE LOST HER POWERS,* SHE WOULDN'T HAVE STOOD A CHANCE AGAINST HIM!

THIS IS MY PROBLEM-- MINE ALONE.

EVER SINCE THAT ALIEN SYMBIOTE JOINED WITH EDDIE BROCK TO FORM VENOM, THEY'VE BEEN ISOLATING ME.

EDDIE THINKS SPIDER-MAN DESTROYED HIS JOURNALISM CAREER, BY EXPOSING HIS BIGGEST STORY AS A LIE!

AND HE'S BLAMED EVERYTHING THAT'S HAPPENED SINCE, INCLUDING THE LOSS OF HIS SANITY, ON ME!

* IN AMAZING SPIDER-MAN #343. -- DANNY

AND AS FOR THE ALIEN, THAT'S AN EVEN STRANGER STORY!
DECAF, PLEASE.
IT WANTED TO MELD WITH ME, BUT I REJECTED IT!
SO THE SCORNED SYMBIOTE JOINED WITH EDDIE, SHARING A HATRED THAT MAKES THEM THE MOST DANGEROUS FOE I'VE EVER FACED!
BECAUSE OF THE SYMBIOTE'S ALIEN NATURE, THEY DON'T EVEN TRIGGER MY EARLY WARNING SPIDER-SENSE!
PASS THE KETCHUP, PAL?
HM? OH, SURE. HERE YOU--
BROCK!
KRISH

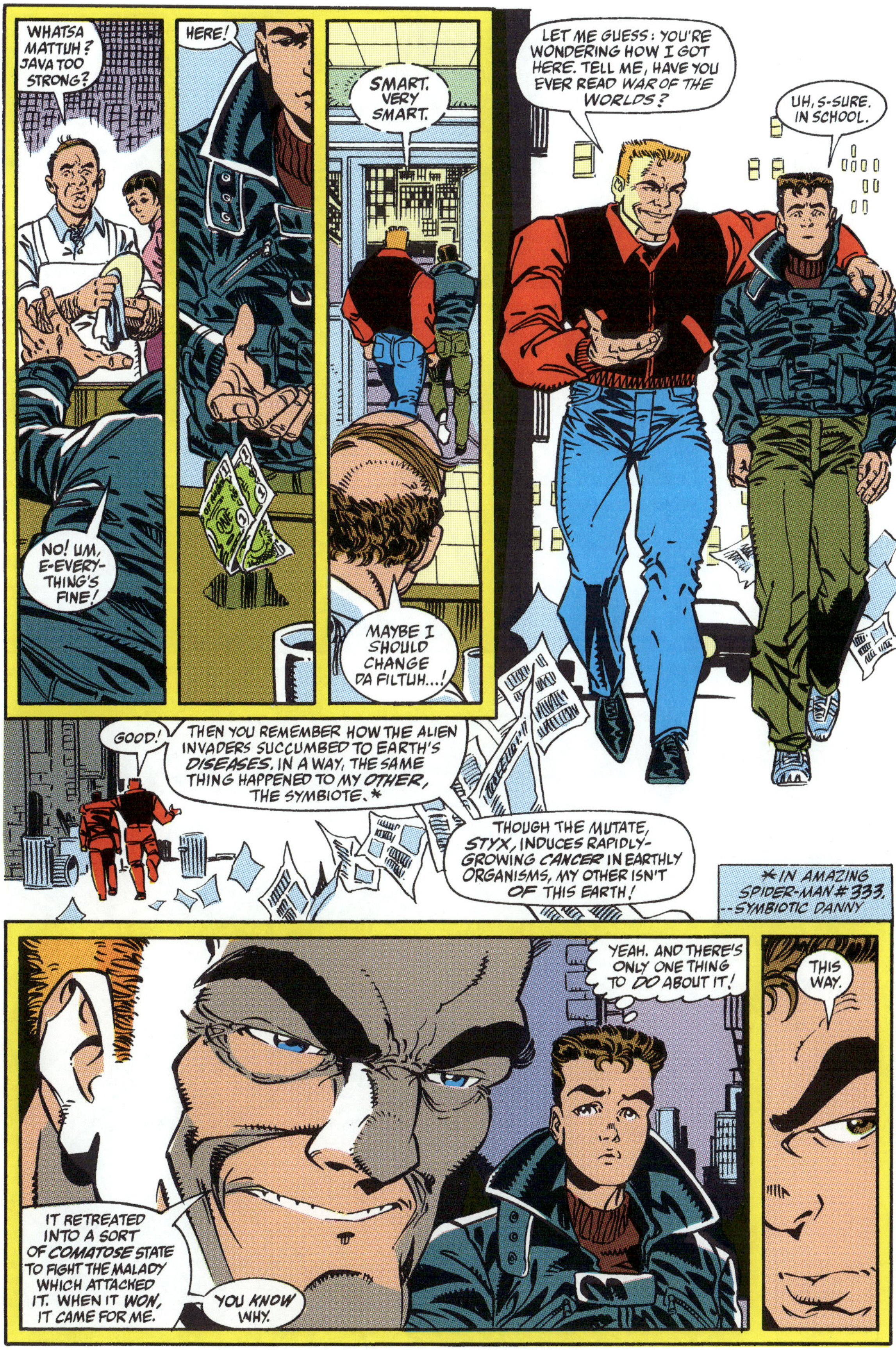

WHATSA MATTUH? JAVA TOO STRONG?
NO! UM. E-EVERY-THING'S FINE!
HERE!
SMART. VERY SMART.
MAYBE I SHOULD CHANGE DA FILTUH...!
LET ME GUESS: YOU'RE WONDERING HOW I GOT HERE. TELL ME, HAVE YOU EVER READ WAR OF THE WORLDS?
UH, S-SURE. IN SCHOOL.
GOOD!
THEN YOU REMEMBER HOW THE ALIEN INVADERS SUCCUMBED TO EARTH'S DISEASES. IN A WAY, THE SAME THING HAPPENED TO MY OTHER, THE SYMBIOTE.*
THOUGH THE MUTATE, STYX, INDUCES RAPIDLY-GROWING CANCER IN EARTHLY ORGANISMS, MY OTHER ISN'T OF THIS EARTH!
*IN AMAZING SPIDER-MAN #333. --SYMBIOTIC DANNY
IT RETREATED INTO A SORT OF COMATOSE STATE TO FIGHT THE MALADY WHICH ATTACKED IT. WHEN IT WON, IT CAME FOR ME.
YOU KNOW WHY.
YEAH. AND THERE'S ONLY ONE THING TO DO ABOUT IT!
THIS WAY.

--COMPLETELY DESERTED!

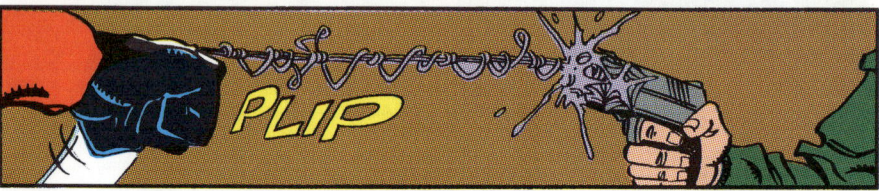

GIMME YER MONEY! ≥sniff≤ NOW!

OH, SWELL!

JUST TAKE IT EASY! HERE'S MY WALLET!

A LOUSY THIRTY BUCKS?! ≥sniff≤ I OUGHTA KILL YA FOR THAT!

HE'S GOING TO KILL ME. OR TRY TO, ANYWAY.

NO.

BUT AT LEAST I CAN TAKE THE BATTLE TO THIS DESERTED ALLEY, SO NO ONE ELSE WILL GET HURT!

PLIP

KRAK

AH, BUT IN NEW YORK, ALLEYWAYS ARE SELDOM--

YOU CAN'T HAVE HIM.
GHIK
HE'S OURS!
eep!
GHYUUUUUUUUh...
FAINTED.
FOR THE BEST, I SUPPOSE.
TOO MANY LIVES HAVE BEEN LOST. THOUGH NOT THE ONE THAT MOST DESERVES--
--eh? GONE.
NO MATTER; WE'RE PATIENT.
AND THERE'S COMFORT IN KNOWING THAT THIS IS, AFTER ALL--
--A SMALL WORLD!

SMALL FAVOR #1: VENOM DOESN'T HAVE A SPIDER-SENSE!
I'VE GOT TO FIND SOME WAY TO PUT VENOM OUT OF COMMISSION!
OR HE WOULD'VE KNOWN I WAS UP HERE, WAITING TO JUMP BACK IN IF HE TRIED TO KILL THAT MUGGER!
BUT THAT DOESN'T CHANGE THE FACT THAT I RAN WHILE THE RUNNING WAS GOOD! AND THAT MAKES ME FEEL TWO FEET TALL!
MORNING.
HOTEL
~YAWN~ FOR THIS I GOT MY THIRTY BUCKS BACK?!
SURE WISH MY MASTERCARD WASN'T CHARGED TO THE MAX! OH, WELL, IF THE COCKROACHES HAVEN'T MADE OFF WITH IT, I SHOULD HAVE SOME CHANGE LEFT.
BETTER USE IT TO CHECK MY--

"--MESSAGES!"

BEEPBEEBOOBIP

--PROFESSOR SWANN, PETER, AT THE UNIVERSITY.

I'VE RECEIVED A REQUEST FROM MOLEED LABS, IN YONKERS.

THEY'VE HAD A BREAKTHROUGH IN CRYOGENICS. THINK THEY MAY BE ABLE TO SAFELY QUICK-FREEZE A HUMAN BEING!

THEY READ THAT PHYSICS PAPER YOU PUBLISHED AND WOULD LIKE YOUR INPUT. INTERESTED? ≥beeep≤

HMMM, EXTRA CREDIT COULDN'T HURT. ANY MORE MESSAGES?

JUST ONE.

HI, PETE. IT'S EDDIE.

SKLAK

HAVE A GOOD NIGHT'S SLEEP?

SONOVA--!

I'VE GOT TO GET THAT-- WAIT! DOC SWANN!

CRYOGENICS!

IF THAT EXPERIMENTAL PROCESS *WORKS*, I COULD ICE VENOM AND SHIP HIM OFF TO THE *ARCTIC*, LIKE THEY DID IN THAT MOVIE, THE BLOB!

IT WOULDN'T KILL HIM, BUT IT WOULD STILL GET HIM OUT OF MY HAIR!

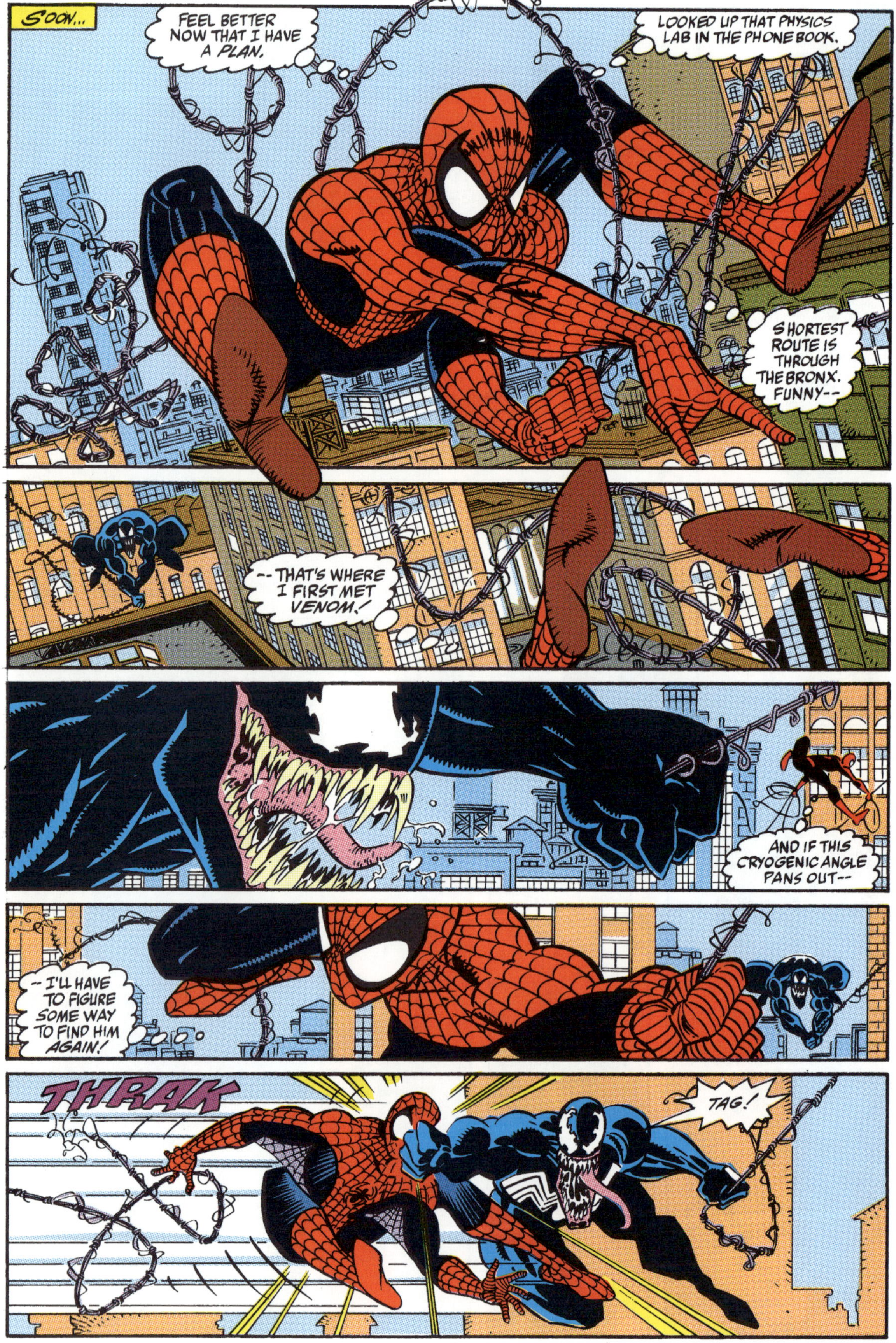
SOON...
FEEL BETTER NOW THAT I HAVE A PLAN.
LOOKED UP THAT PHYSICS LAB IN THE PHONE BOOK.
SHORTEST ROUTE IS THROUGH THE BRONX. FUNNY--
--THAT'S WHERE I FIRST MET VENOM!
AND IF THIS CRYOGENIC ANGLE PANS OUT--
--I'LL HAVE TO FIGURE SOME WAY TO FIND HIM AGAIN!
THRAK
TAG!

WHUMP
NNF
TAP
BLAST! I HATE NOT BEING ABLE TO USE MY SPIDER-SENSE! I NEVER KNOW WHERE THAT GUY WILL TURN UP NEX-- huh?
YOU'RE IT!
WHOK
CASE IN POINT...!
SKRRRRIIIKKK
GOT TO DIG IN! SLOW MY FALL! WAIT FOR VENOM'S NEXT MOVE AND--
NO PEEKING!
--USE IT AGAINST HIM!
CHEATER, CHEATER, GRADE REPEATER!
CHUNCH

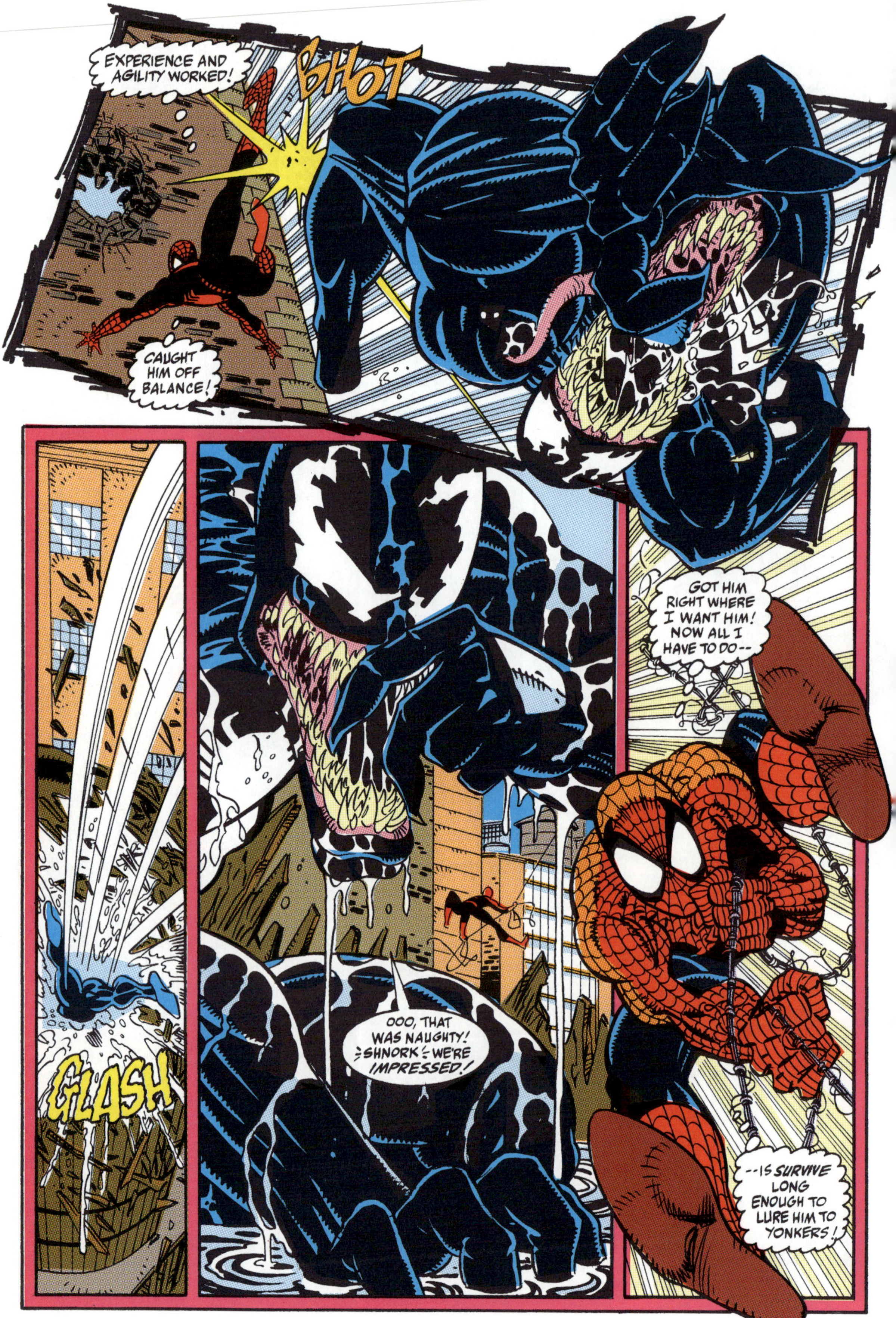
EXPERIENCE AND AGILITY WORKED!
SHOT
CAUGHT HIM OFF BALANCE!
GLASH
OOO, THAT WAS NAUGHTY! SHNORK WE'RE IMPRESSED!
GOT HIM RIGHT WHERE I WANT HIM! NOW ALL I HAVE TO DO--
--IS SURVIVE LONG ENOUGH TO LURE HIM TO YONKERS!

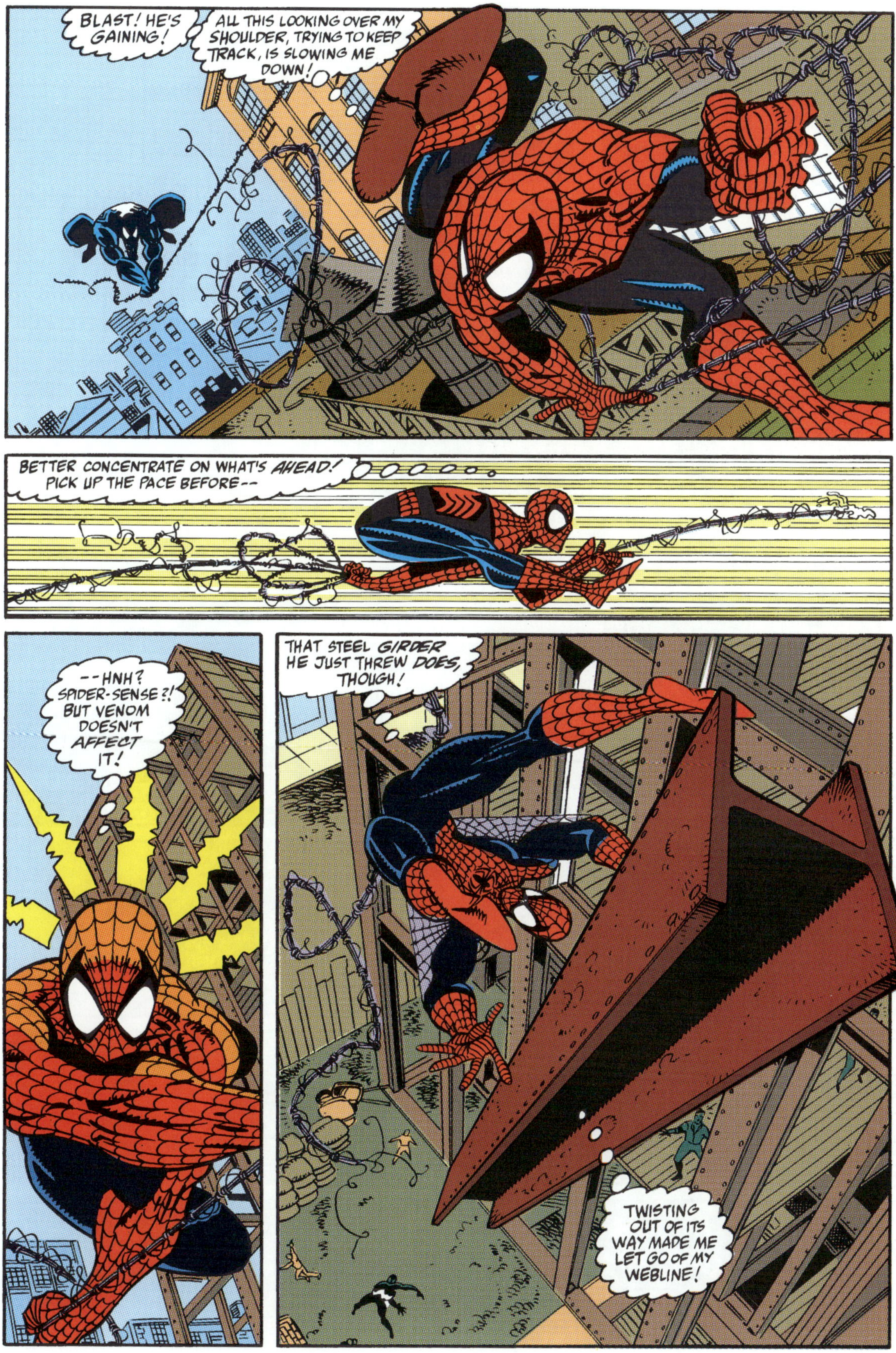
BLAST! HE'S GAINING!
ALL THIS LOOKING OVER MY SHOULDER, TRYING TO KEEP TRACK, IS SLOWING ME DOWN!
BETTER CONCENTRATE ON WHAT'S AHEAD! PICK UP THE PACE BEFORE--
--HNH? SPIDER-SENSE?! BUT VENOM DOESN'T AFFECT IT!
THAT STEEL GIRDER HE JUST THREW DOES, THOUGH!
TWISTING OUT OF ITS WAY MADE ME LET GO OF MY WEBLINE!

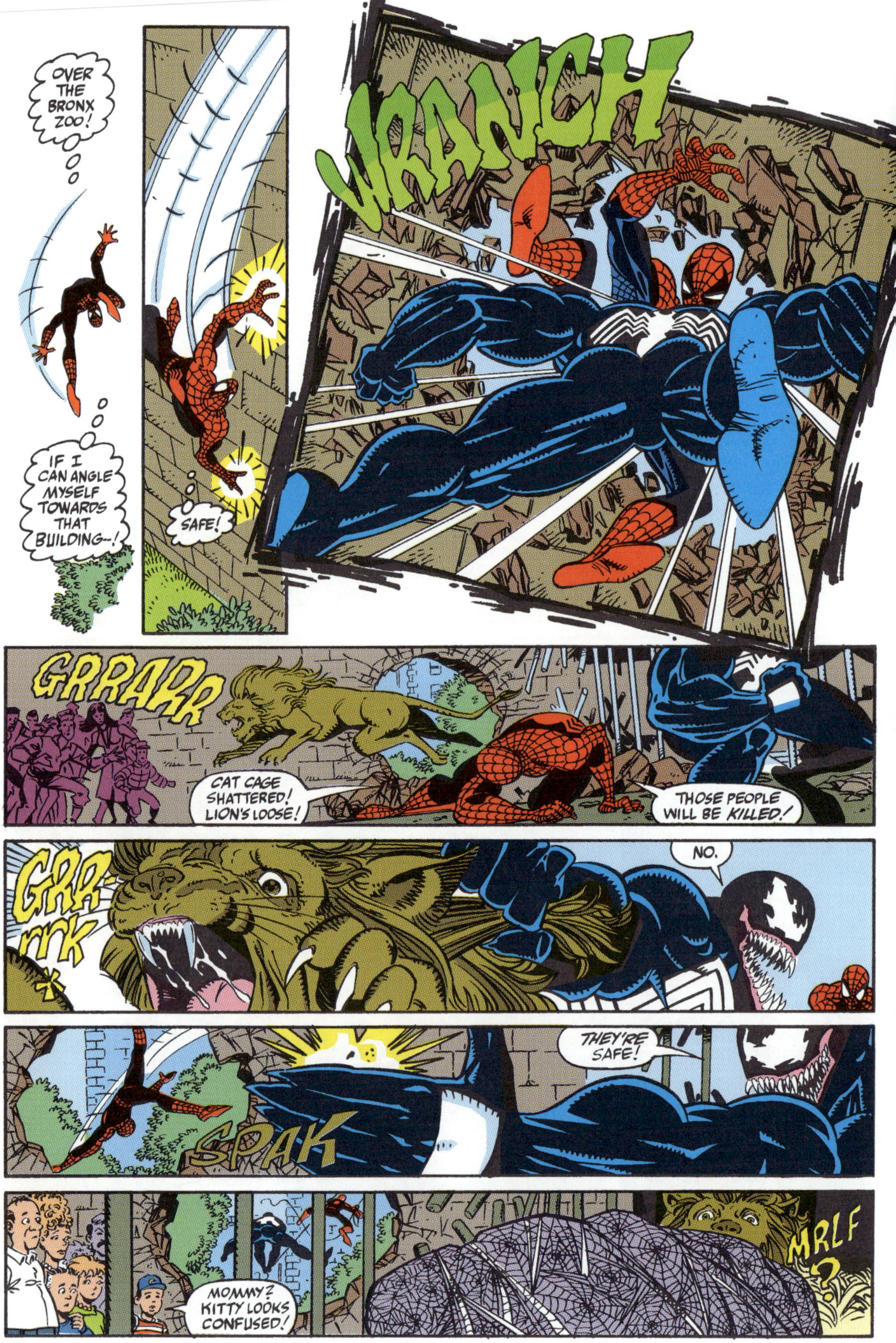

OVER THE BRONX ZOO!
IF I CAN ANGLE MYSELF TOWARDS THAT BUILDING--!
SAFE!
WRANCH
GRRARR
CAT CAGE SHATTERED! LION'S LOOSE!
THOSE PEOPLE WILL BE KILLED!
GRR-rrrk
NO.
THEY'RE SAFE!
SPAK
MOMMY? KITTY LOOKS CONFUSED!
MRLF ?

NO QUESTION.
I'M GETTING MY BUTT WHIPPED! IF I DON'T TAKE THE OFFENSIVE--
--I WON'T MAKE IT TO YONKERS!
THUS...
DISAPPEARED? OH, GOODY!
WE LOVE HIDE AND SEEK!
AND SHRED!
AND DISMEMBER...!
DISMEMBER THIS, YOU--
FWOK

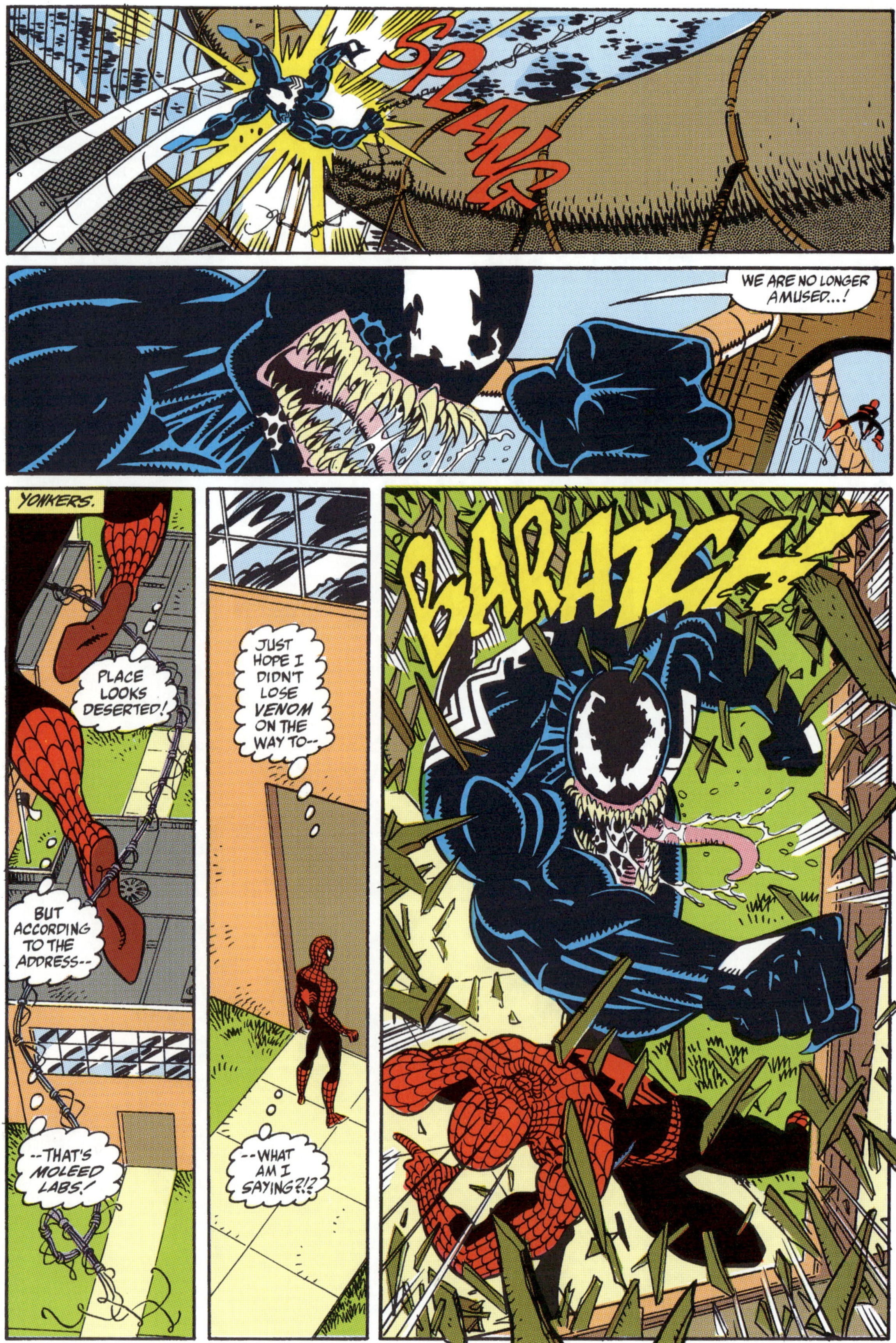
SPLANG
WE ARE NO LONGER AMUSED...!
YONKERS.
PLACE LOOKS DESERTED!
BUT ACCORDING TO THE ADDRESS--
--THAT'S MOLEED LABS!
JUST HOPE I DIDN'T LOSE VENOM ON THE WAY TO--
--WHAT AM I SAYING?!?
BARATCH!

EVEN WITHOUT MY SPIDER-SENSE--
--I COULD SEE THAT COMING A MILE AWAY!
JUST AS EMPTY INSIDE! WHERE IS EVERYBODY?
MORE IMPORTANTLY, WHERE ARE THE LABS?
WHEW AT LAST!
HEY, BUDDY! WHERE'S THE CRYOGENICS SECTION?
DOWN THERE?
THANKS!
THINK NOTHING OF IT!
PLEASE!

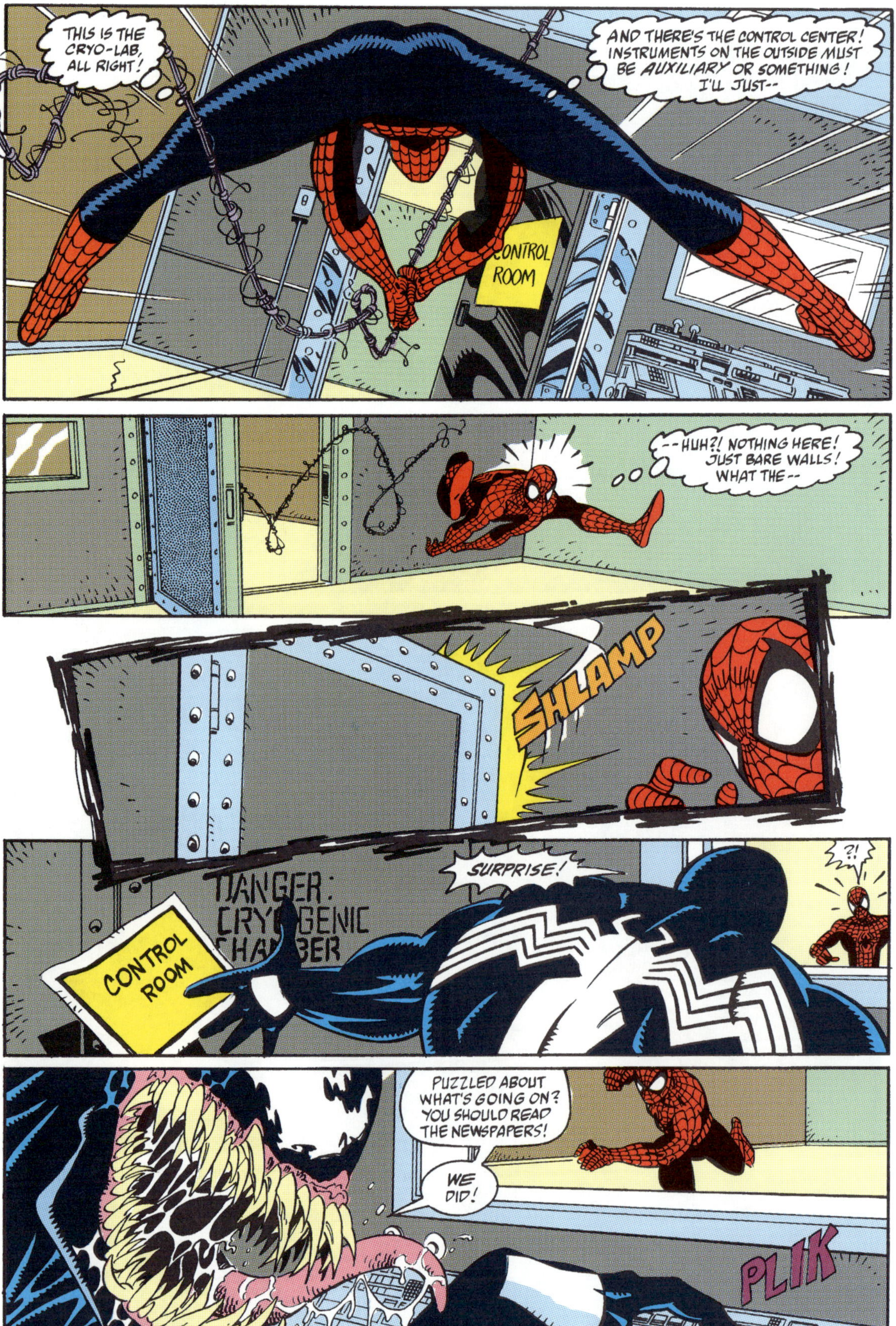
THIS IS THE CRYO-LAB, ALL RIGHT!
AND THERE'S THE CONTROL CENTER! INSTRUMENTS ON THE OUTSIDE MUST BE AUXILIARY OR SOMETHING! I'LL JUST--
CONTROL ROOM
--HUH?! NOTHING HERE! JUST BARE WALLS! WHAT THE--
SHLAMP
SURPRISE!
?!
DANGER: CRYOGENIC CHAMBER
CONTROL ROOM
PUZZLED ABOUT WHAT'S GOING ON? YOU SHOULD READ THE NEWSPAPERS!
WE DID!
PLIK

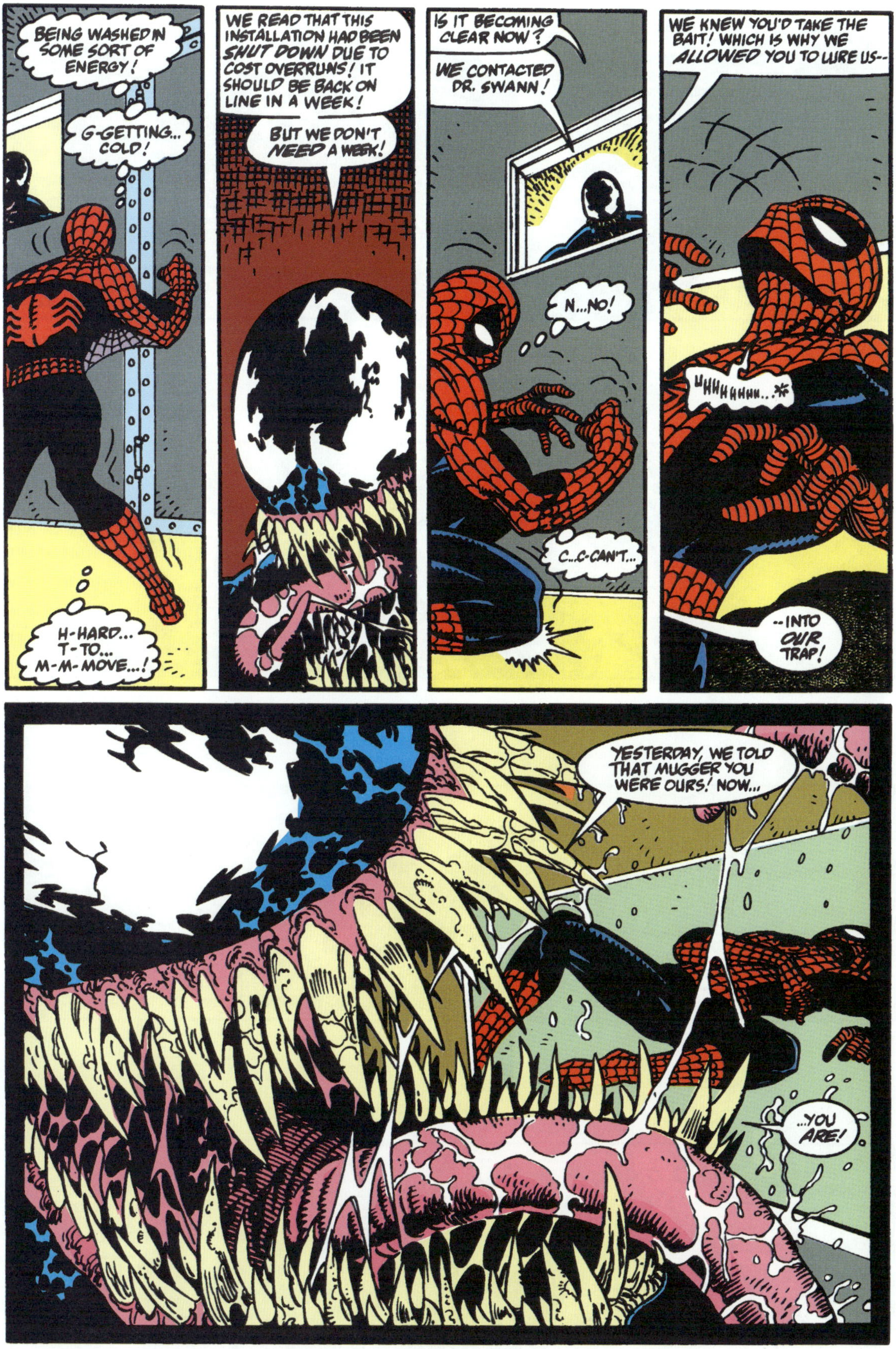
BEING WASHED IN SOME SORT OF ENERGY!
G-GETTING... COLD!
H-HARD... T-TO... M-M-MOVE...!
WE READ THAT THIS INSTALLATION HAD BEEN SHUT DOWN DUE TO COST OVERRUNS! IT SHOULD BE BACK ON LINE IN A WEEK!
BUT WE DON'T NEED A WEEK!
IS IT BECOMING CLEAR NOW?
WE CONTACTED DR. SWANN!
N...NO!
C...C-CAN'T...
WE KNEW YOU'D TAKE THE BAIT! WHICH IS WHY WE ALLOWED YOU TO LURE US--
UHHHHHHH...*
--INTO OUR TRAP!
YESTERDAY, WE TOLD THAT MUGGER YOU WERE OURS! NOW...
...YOU ARE!

CHAPTER FOUR

HE'S COLD. QUIVERING, SHAKING, TEETH-CHATTERING COLD.

WHICH DOESN'T SEEM ALL THAT UNREASONABLE.

SINCE HIS LAST MEMORY IS OF BEING CRYOGENICALLY *QUICK-FROZEN* AT AN EXPERIMENTAL LAB, COURTESY OF *VENOM!*

BUT AS HE SWIMS BACK TO CONSCIOUSNESS THROUGH A CHILL, VISION-BLURRING HAZE, HE HAS ONE QUESTION: IF HE'S SO COLD--

--HOW COME HE'S *SWEATING?*

SUN!

SEARING!

HOT AS AUGUST!

THAWING ME OUT!

AND... WATER? WAVES?

HAVE TO CONCENTRATE! FOCUS! GET TO MY FEET AND--

--SAND! A BEACH?! THIS CAN'T BE YONKERS!

WHERE THE BLAZES AM I?!

WHY, YOU'RE IN *PARADISE*, SPIDER-MAN! CAN YOU THINK OF A BETTER PLACE--

--TO DIE?

THE BONEYARD HOP!

"PARADISE IS *PERFECT*, ISN'T IT?

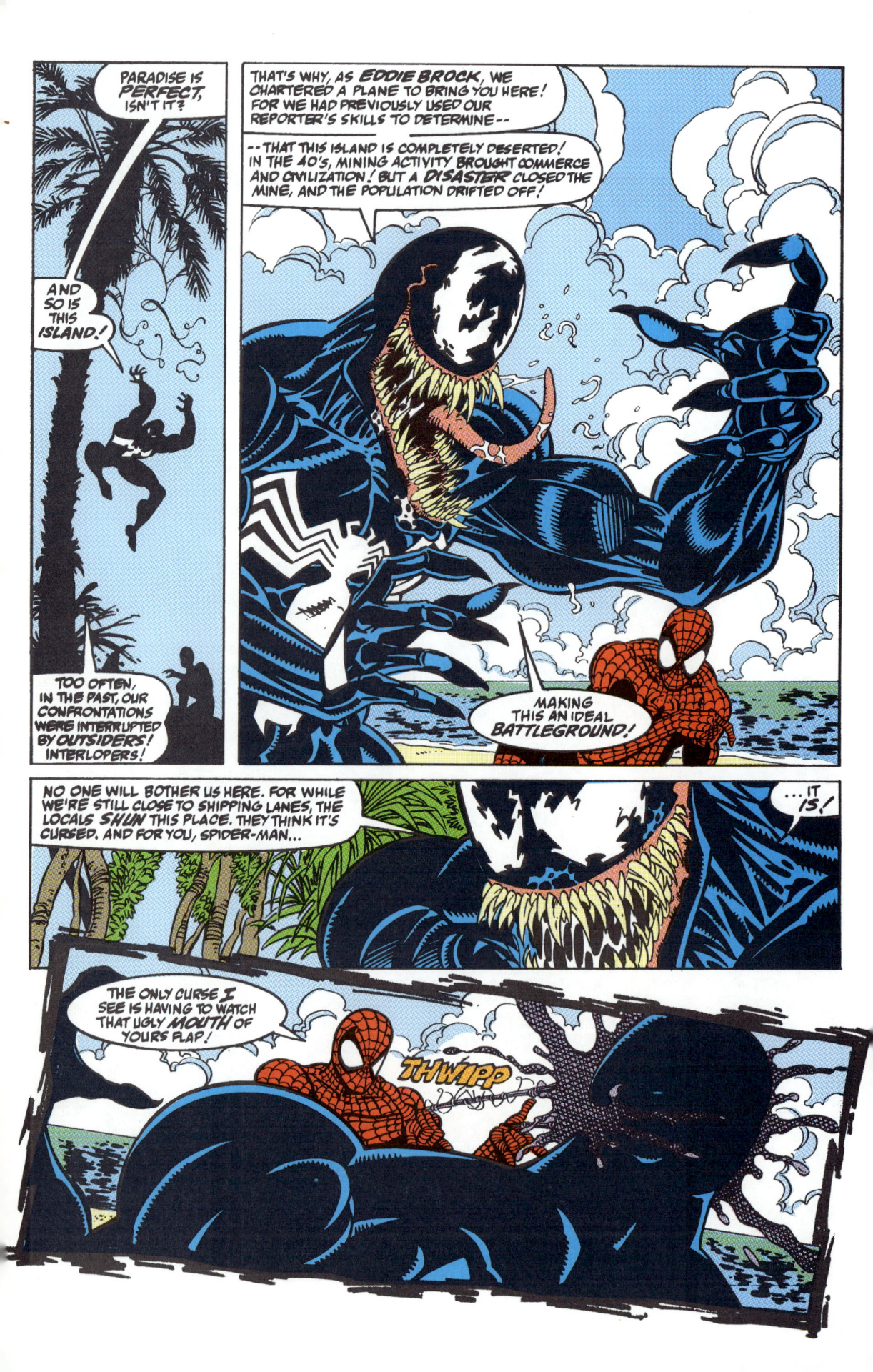

AND SO IS THIS *ISLAND!*

TOO OFTEN, IN THE PAST, OUR CONFRONTATIONS WERE INTERRUPTED BY *OUTSIDERS!* INTERLOPERS!

THAT'S WHY, AS *EDDIE BROCK*, WE CHARTERED A PLANE TO BRING YOU HERE! FOR WE HAD PREVIOUSLY USED OUR REPORTER'S SKILLS TO DETERMINE--

--THAT THIS ISLAND IS COMPLETELY DESERTED! IN THE 40'S, MINING ACTIVITY BROUGHT COMMERCE AND CIVILIZATION! BUT A *DISASTER* CLOSED THE MINE, AND THE POPULATION DRIFTED OFF!

MAKING THIS AN IDEAL *BATTLEGROUND!*

...IT *IS!*

NO ONE WILL BOTHER US HERE. FOR WHILE WE'RE STILL CLOSE TO SHIPPING LANES, THE LOCALS *SHUN* THIS PLACE. THEY THINK IT'S CURSED. AND FOR YOU, SPIDER-MAN...

THE ONLY CURSE *I* SEE IS HAVING TO WATCH THAT UGLY *MOUTH* OF YOURS FLAP!

THWIPP

WEBBING WON'T STOP HIM, BUT MAYBE IT'LL BUY SOME TIME! I'M STILL WEAK, FUZZY! HAVE TO GET MYSELF TOGETHER--
-- FAST!
NO FOOLIN'!
SHRRRIIIIP
♪NOW THIS IS A TALE OF OUR CASTAWAYS, THEY'RE HERE FOR A LONG LONG TIIIIIIIME!♪
HEH HEH HEH

JUNGLE? GRAPEVINES? WHAT NEXT?
A CHIMP SIDEKICK?
C'MON, PETER! FREEZING AND RELOCATION WERE TRAUMATIC, BUT YOU'VE GOT TO SNAP OUT OF IT!
REMEMBER HOW THAT ALIEN SYMBIOTE MELDED WITH EDDIE BROCK TO FORM VENOM!
HOW THE ONLY THING EITHER OF THEM REALLY WANTS IS TO MAKE YOU DEAD!
VENOM WAS RIGHT WHEN HE SAID OTHER PEOPLE SHOWING UP HAS SAVED MY BUTT: THE POLICE, STYX AND STONE...!
THEIR INTERVENTION CHANGED THE ODDS IN MY FAVOR!
AND TWO OTHER THINGS TO REMEMBER: VENOM IS INSANE. HIS THOUGHT PROCESSES AREN'T LIKE A NORMAL HUMAN'S! PLUS--
--THIS IS HIS TURF. HE RE-SEARCHED IT, PROBABLY SCOUTED IT BEFOREHAND. HE COULD BE--
--ANYWHERE?

≥GHLK≤

PLOOSH

INTERLUDE: PITTSBURGH, WHERE THE SUN ALSO SHINES -- THOUGH NOT IN THE HEART OF MARY JANE WATSON-PARKER.

I KNOW HE SENT ME HERE SO I'D BE SAFE WHILE HE WENT AFTER VENOM.

FLUP

TOMMY AND KEVIN. SWEETEST NEPHEWS A GAL COULD HAVE. SO CAREFREE.

BUT I CAN'T STAND IT MUCH LONGER! NOT KNOWING IF HE'S--

HA, HA! AUNT MARY JANE'S ALL WET!

CAN'T EVEN GUESS THEIR UNCLE PETER MIGHT BE DYING AT THIS VERY MOMENT!

THAT WASN'T FUNNY, BLAST IT! I OUGHTA TAN YOUR LITTLE--

G-G-GOSH, AUNT MARY JANE! W-WE'RE SORRY!

WHAT AM I DOING? THEY DIDN'T MEAN ANY HARM!
GOT TO KEEP IT TOGETHER! BE STRONG!
FOR PETER!
LOOK, GUYS, IF YOU'RE GONNA LOB SNOWBALLS, DON'T AIM AT THE HEAD, OKAY? SOMEONE COULD GET HURT!
NOW LET'S FINISH "FROSTY" AND BREAK FOR SOME COCOA, HUH?
ALL RIIIIGHT!
MEANWHILE...
THAT'S A NEW TRICK! BUT I SHOULD HAVE ANTICIPATED IT! THE SYMBIOTE CAN EMULATE CLOTHES, SKIN... WHY NOT WATER? =UNF=
BETTER GRAB THAT SUNKEN BRANCH! 'CAUSE IT SEEMS THERE'S ONE OTHER THING THAT COSTUME CAN DO THAT I CAN'T!
SPUNK

BLAPSH
BREATHE UNDER WATER!
GHASP
THWIP
MADE IT!
THIS TIME...!
FIRST BLOOD--
--QUITE LITERALLY--
--IS OURS!
YUM!
SSSLURP

ABANDONED VILLAGE! HAS TO BE WHERE THOSE *MINERS* WERE *HOUSED* BEFORE THE *DISASTER!*

AND THAT *GRAVEYARD* MUST BE WHERE THEY WERE *BURIED!*

WHERE *I'LL* BE BURIED UNLESS I THINK FAST!

HMM, MY OLD BUDDY, FLASH THOMPSON, WAS AN EAGLE SCOUT IN HIGH SCHOOL! WON A LOT OF MERIT BADGES.

HE TRIED TO TEACH ME SOME SCOUTING TRICKS. SURE HOPE I CAN REMEMBER THOSE LESSONS! 'CAUSE THE BADGE I'M GOING FOR--

--IS MY *LIFE!*

EVENTUALLY...

ALL SET! NOW I JUST HAVE TO LURE VENOM HERE! BUT HOW?

IN THE PAST, HE *USUALLY* FOUND *ME!* AND -- WAITAMINIT! "*USUALLY*"?

HE...

...ALWAYS...

...FOUND ME!

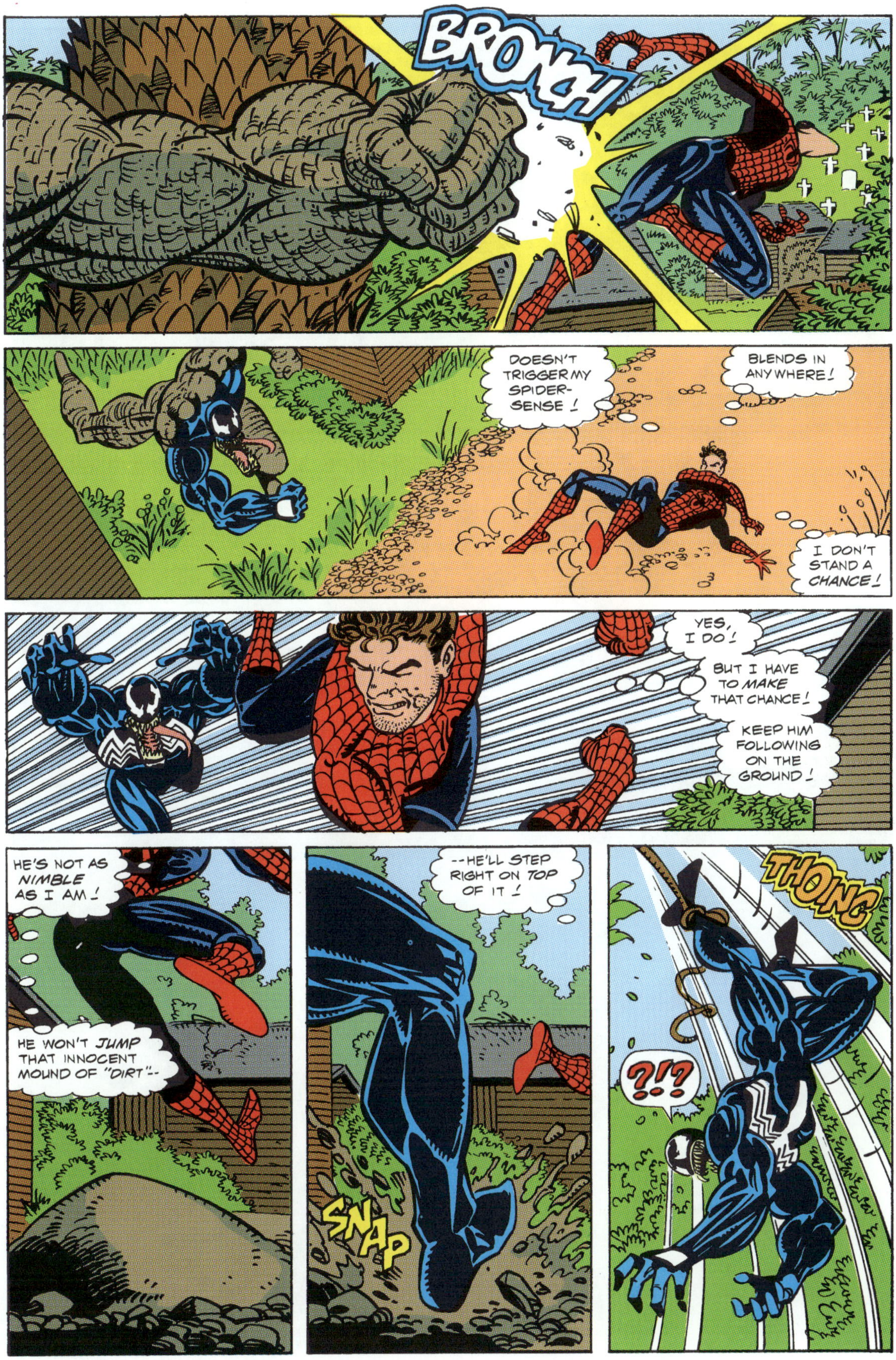
BRONCH
DOESN'T TRIGGER MY SPIDER-SENSE!
BLENDS IN ANYWHERE!
I DON'T STAND A CHANCE!
YES, I DO!
BUT I HAVE TO MAKE THAT CHANCE!
KEEP HIM FOLLOWING ON THE GROUND!
HE'S NOT AS NIMBLE AS I AM!
HE WON'T JUMP THAT INNOCENT MOUND OF "DIRT"--
--HE'LL STEP RIGHT ON TOP OF IT!
SNAP
THOING
?!?

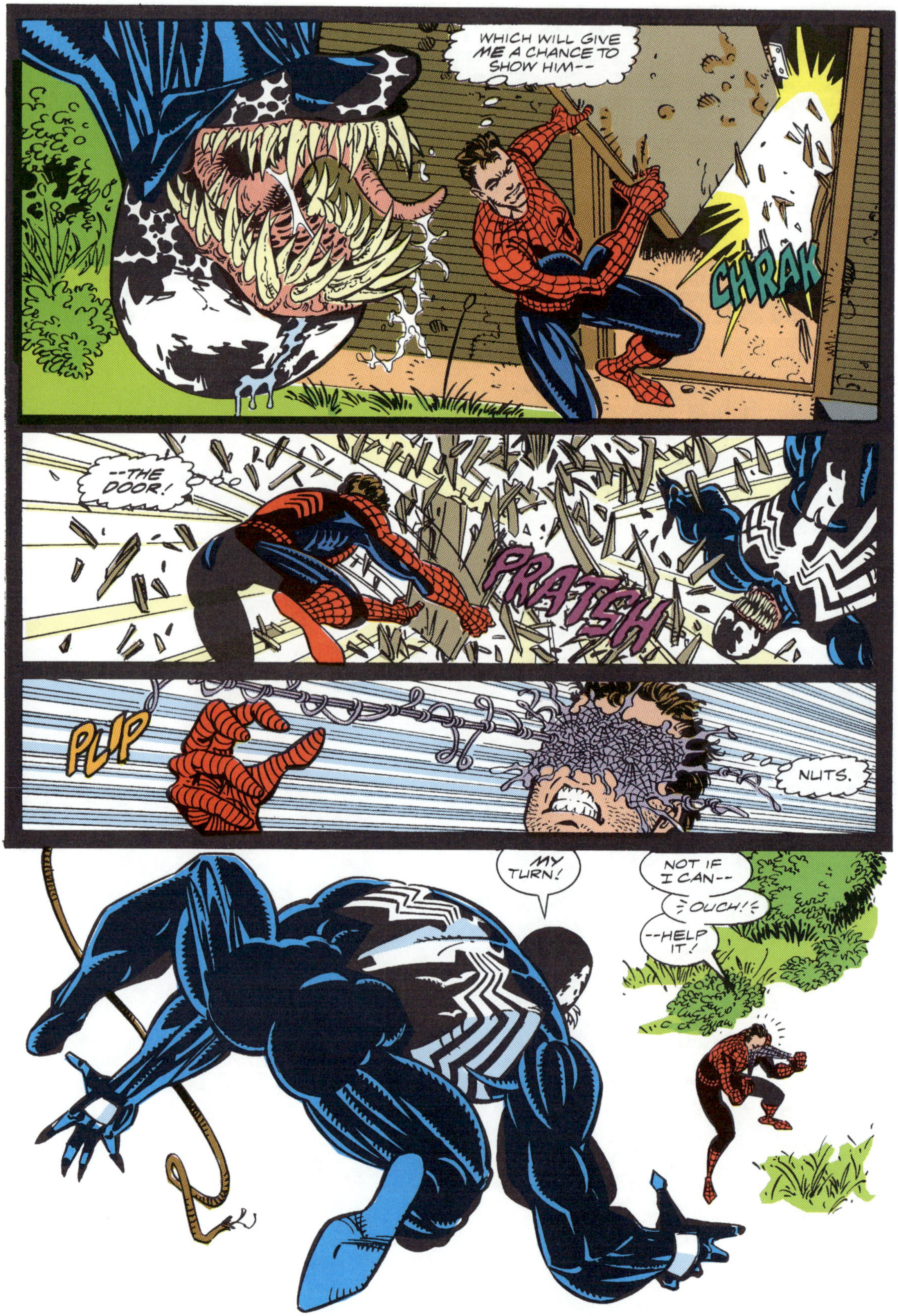
WHICH WILL GIVE ME A CHANCE TO SHOW HIM--
CHRAK
--THE DOOR!
PRATSH
PLIP
NUTS.
MY TURN!
NOT IF I CAN--
OUCH!
--HELP IT!

OOO, RUNNING IN TERROR!
NICE STRATEGY!
MOVING TARGETS ARE FUN!
SSSWISH
EEP! BARELY TWISTED OUT OF THE WAY! LOST HOLD OF MY WEBLINE! GOT TO--
--HUH? TRUCK FALLING INTO THE GROUND?!
AND IT'S NOT THE ONLY ONE!
THIS ISN'T A HOLE--IT'S THAT ABANDONED MINE!
K-KOFF! GHAK!
NOW I KNOW WHAT CAUSED THE DISASTER VENOM TALKED ABOUT!

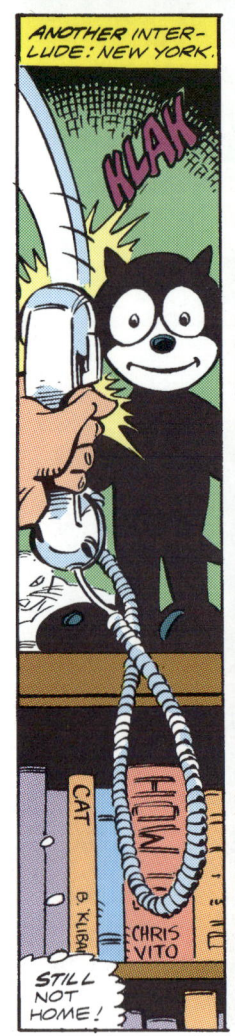

GAS! THIS PLACE IS *FULL* OF IT!

MUST HAVE EXPLODED, S-STARTED A CAVE-IN! HAVE TO GET *OUT* OF HERE, OR I'M--

--*DEAD!*

ANOTHER INTERLUDE: NEW YORK.

KLAK

STILL NOT HOME!

LET'S HUSTLE IT, HUH, BABE? WE'LL BE LATE FOR THE CONCERT!

I, UM, I'M NOT FEELING SO HOT, FLASH. MAYBE YOU SHOULD GO ON.

C'MON, FELICIA, IT TOOK ME *WEEKS* TO GET THESE HYPNO-LOVEWHEEL TICKETS!

THEN DON'T GO AT *ALL*, BLAST IT!

I DIDN'T SUFFER ALL THAT HASSLE JUST TO GO *STAG!*

OHHH... FLASH DIDN'T DESERVE THAT! I'M JUST WORRIED ABOUT PETER TRYING TO SURVIVE VENOM! WITHOUT MY BLACK CAT POWERS--
--THERE ISN'T A BLOODY THING I CAN DO TO HELP HIM!
GUESS I STILL HAVE FEELINGS FOR HIM, EVEN THOUGH MY MAIN AFFECTIONS BELONG TO--
--FLASH? YEAH. THEY DO!
HOLD UP, CHAMP! I'VE CHANGED MY MIND!
ALL RIGHT!
SORRY, SPIDER. I HAVE A LIFE TO LEAD. I GUESS... YOU'RE ON YOUR OWN.
I'M ON MY OWN!
GOT TO GET MYSELF OUT OF THIS! SNAG THOSE ROTTED CEILING SUPPORTS, AND INVITE VENOM--
THWIP
--TO COME ON DOWN!
KRRRRRIK

COAST IS CLEAR!
YECH! SMELLS BAD!
WE DON'T LIKE STINKY PLACES!
JUST FOR THAT--
--WE'RE GOING TO EAT YOUR LUNGS!
BETTER CONSERVE MY WEBBING CARTRIDGES! THERE'S NO WAY TO REFILL THEM ONCE THEY'RE--
--EH?
A BOAT! VENOM SAID WE WERE CLOSE TO SHIPPING LANES!
ALL I HAVE TO DO IS USE MY SPIDER-STRENGTH TO SWIM OUT TO IT AND I'M--

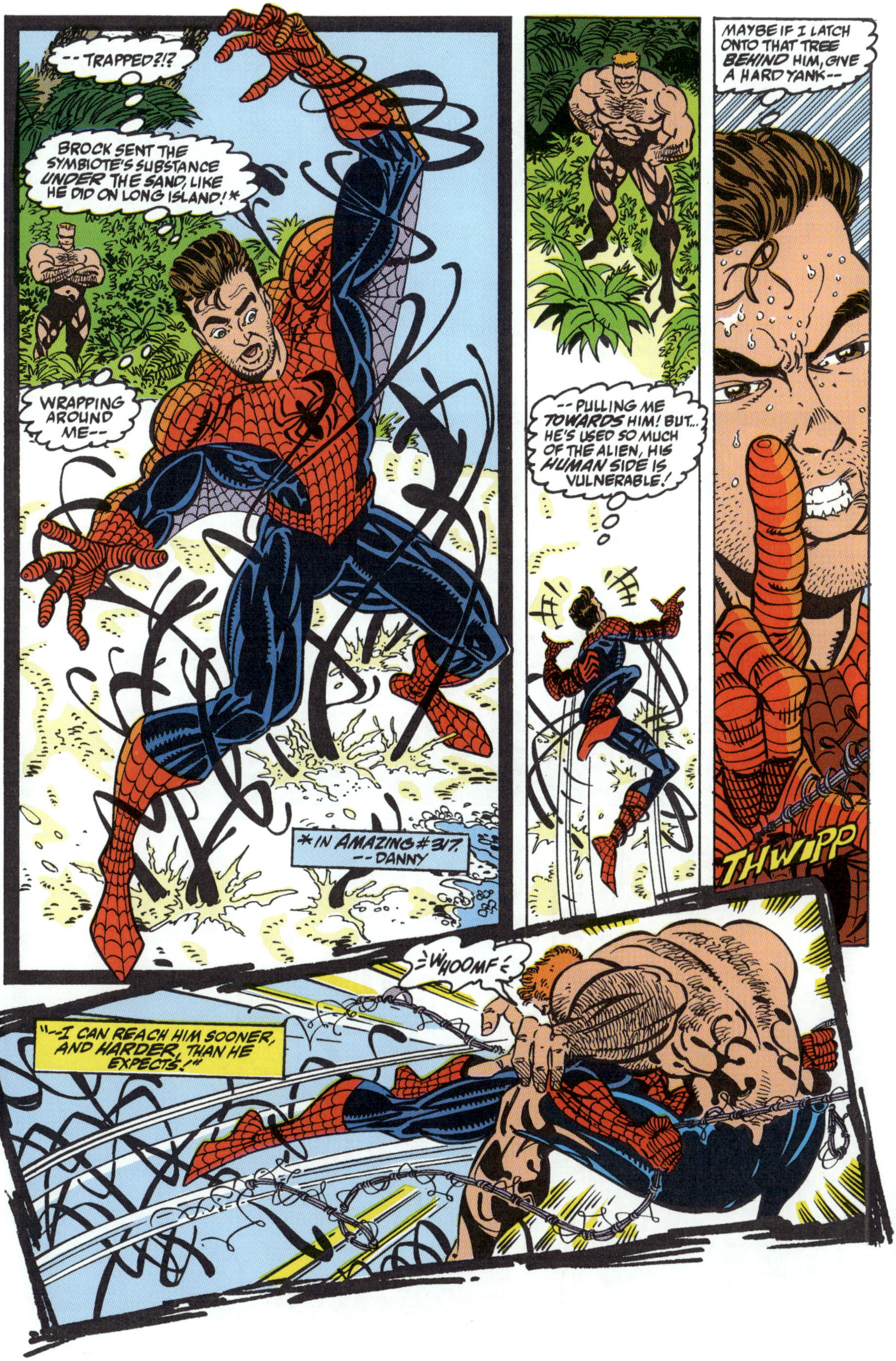
--TRAPPED?!?
BROCK SENT THE SYMBIOTE'S SUBSTANCE UNDER THE SAND, LIKE HE DID ON LONG ISLAND!*
WRAPPING AROUND ME--
*IN AMAZING #317. --DANNY
--PULLING ME TOWARDS HIM! BUT... HE'S USED SO MUCH OF THE ALIEN, HIS HUMAN SIDE IS VULNERABLE!
MAYBE IF I LATCH ONTO THAT TREE BEHIND HIM, GIVE A HARD YANK--
THWIPP
WHOOMF
"--I CAN REACH HIM SOONER, AND HARDER, THAN HE EXPECTS!"

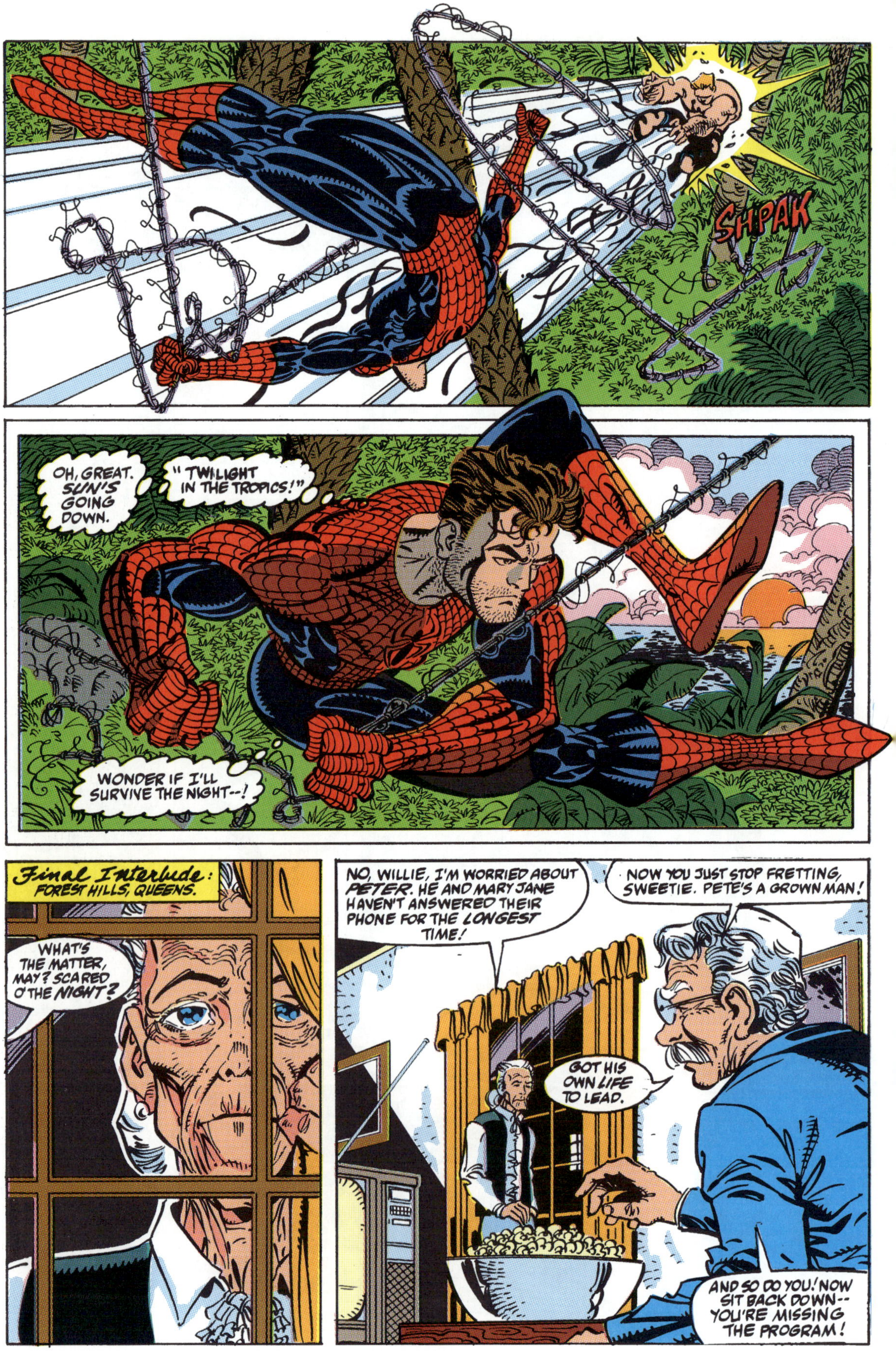
SHPAK
OH, GREAT. SUN'S GOING DOWN.
"TWILIGHT IN THE TROPICS!"
WONDER IF I'LL SURVIVE THE NIGHT--!
Final Interlude: FOREST HILLS, QUEENS.
WHAT'S THE MATTER, MAY? SCARED O'THE NIGHT?
NO, WILLIE, I'M WORRIED ABOUT PETER. HE AND MARY JANE HAVEN'T ANSWERED THEIR PHONE FOR THE LONGEST TIME!
NOW YOU JUST STOP FRETTING, SWEETIE. PETE'S A GROWN MAN!
GOT HIS OWN LIFE TO LEAD.
AND SO DO YOU! NOW SIT BACK DOWN-- YOU'RE MISSING THE PROGRAM!

"I GUESS YOU'RE RIGHT. I DO WORRY TOO MUCH!"

"I'M SURE PETER'S FINE."

"THAT'S MY GAL! NOW SCRUNCH IN CLOSE--"

"-- THE SHOW'S JUST STARTIN'!"

"TSK! HOW DO THOSE FLY GIRLS MOVE LIKE THAT?"

"HAVE TO MOVE CAREFULLY! I'D FEEL BETTER WEBSWINGING--"

"-- BUT I'M DOWN TO MY LAST WEBBING CARTRIDGES!"

"AND I'D BETTER SAVE THEM IN CASE -- HUH? FOOT SINKING INTO THE GROUND! WHAT--"

"AH, GEEZ! SHALLOW GRAVE, F-FILLED WITH ROTTING BONES! JUST WHAT I NEEDED TO KEEP ME CALM!"

"WHAT NEXT? AN EERIE LIGHT OUT IN THE--"

"-- JUNGLE?"

EASY, BOY! THIS ISN'T A STEPHEN KING NOVEL!
THAT LIGHT COULD BE YOUR SALVATION!
MIGHT MEAN THERE'S SOMEONE ELSE ON THIS ISLAND BESIDES--
--VENOM.
RIGHT.
LIKE MY LUCK SHOULD CHANGE!
EDDIE'S JUST TAKING A BREATHER, WHILE THE ALIEN KEEPS WATCH!
FACE IT, PILGRIM: THEY'RE IMPLACABLE! THERE ISN'T A THING THAT WILL KEEP THEM FROM COMING AFTER--
--WAIT! I FORGOT. THERE IS ONE THING THAT WILL STOP THEM. THE ONLY THING THEY REALLY WANT:
MY DEATH!
AN HOUR PASSES... FILLED WITH PREPARATION... AND FOLLOWED BY--
WHU--?!
THWIP

WALL-CRAWLER KNOWS FIRE *REPELS* YOU!
PROBABLY THINKS TO USE IT *AGAINST* US! THAT WILL BE THE *LAST* THOUGHT HE HAS--
--BEFORE WE SQUISH HIS *BRAIN* INTO CRIMSON GREASE!
EVERYTHING RIDES ON BROCK'S INSANITY, THE *RAGE* IT PRODUCES!
GOT TO KEEP HIM ANGRY, *RE-ACTING* INSTEAD OF REASONING!
AND JUST HOPE THOSE REACTIONS ARE CONSISTENT WITH HIS *PAST* BEHAVIOR!
LAST OF MY WEBBING! NOT THAT IT MATTERS! 'CAUSE IF THIS DOESN'T WORK--
--I WON'T BE GETTING A *SECOND* CHANCE!
THWI-WIP
EEYEEGH! STICKY!
HOLDING US BACK!
THAT'S NOT--

SHRIPT

--NICE!

BUT WE DON'T HAVE TO REACH YOU TO SMASH YOU!

WE CAN STILL SEE THE LIGHT FROM YOUR TORCH!

TARGET ENOUGH TO SEND THIS RUSTING VAN--

--DEAD ON! WE HIT HIM!

TORCH... FALLING TO THE GROUND!

Falling... UNDER THE GROUND?

PABWABOOM

?!?

AHHH, YES! THE MINE! THE GAS!

THE... TORCH!

HIS GRIN IS GHASTLY, MADE ALL THE MORE SO BY A THICK DROOL OF SATISFACTION.

Panel 1: AN EMOTION THAT SWELLS, EVEN AS, THE NEXT MORNING, THE GAS-FED FLAMES FINALLY FADE.

CHARRED BONES... SCRAPS OF COSTUME... A MELTED WEB-SHOOTER?

IT'S *TRUE!* SWEET PROVIDENCE, WE *DID* IT!

Panel 2: ALAS, SPIDER-MAN, BANE OF OUR EXISTENCE...

...YOU'RE *DEAD*, YOU SON OF A *MONKEY!*

HA HA HA HA HA HA!

Panel 3: ANOTHER SHIP! 'BOUT *TIME!* BEEN TREADING WATER FOR *HOURS!*

TOSSED MY COSTUME AND WEB-SHOOTERS INTO THAT MINE CRATER, THEN WEDGED THE TORCH IN A BRANCH ABOVE IT!

VENOM TOOK THE BAIT, *AND* THAT VAN I PLANTED! FOR ONCE--

--HIS MADNESS WORKED *FOR* ME!

Panel 4: THE MADNESS IS *OVER*, NO LONGER IS THERE A REASON FOR VENOM TO EXIST!

SHALL WE REMAIN HERE, THEN?

WE HAVE FOOD, WATER-- BLESSED PEACE.

WHY *NOT* STAY? BE HAPPY?

Panel 5: ≷SIGH≷ WHAT A WONDERFUL *FEELING* IT IS...

Panel 6: "...TO BE *FREE!*"

This Venom tale occurred before our previous story. After a daring escape from authorities, Eddie made his way cross-country by hitchhiking, his final destination being a confrontation with Spider-Man!

During a nasty blizzard, Brock hooked up with a young family, who let him ride with them in their van. After hours of traveling, they pulled into a small diner for a bite to eat. When a band of armed robbers stormed on to the scene, Venom was cast in the role of lethal protector for the first time...

RURAL MISSOURI, JUST OFF I-44.
TRUCKSTOPS HAVE THE BEST FOOD AROUND, HON! THAT'S WHY ALL THE TRUCKERS EAT HERE!
ON'S DINER
RIGHT, MR. BROCK?
UH, SURE, CHUCK.
NOTE: THIS STORY TAKES PLACE BETWEEN AMAZING SPIDER-MAN #'s 315 & 316. --DANNY
ACTUALLY, THEY STOP HERE 'CAUSE THE LOTS ARE BIG ENOUGH FOR THEIR 18-WHEELERS! BUT WHY ARGUE?
THESE FOLKS WERE NICE ENOUGH TO GIVE ME A RIDE, AND I DON'T WANT ANYTHING TO SPOIL THEIR--
OPEN
PAT 'EM DOWN, JAKE! THEY MAKE ONE STUPID MOVE--
--KILL 'EM ALL!
DONUT JOY 50
TRUCKSTOP of DOOM!
WHAT TH--?

D-DON'T WORRY, ELLEN! I-I'LL PROTECT YOU AND LITTLE BOBBY!
YOU'RE MAKING A BIG MISTAKE, FRIEND!
PLEASE! DON'T START ANY TROUBLE! IF WE JUST LEAVE THEM ALONE, THEY'LL GO AWAY!
YOU GOTTA BE KIDDING.
NO! I OVERHEARD THEIR LEADER, GUY CALLED SPANGLE! HE SAID THEY'RE JUST AFTER MONEY!
TODAY'S SPECIAL
BUT WE DON'T HAVE--
NOT FROM YOU! THE WEEKLY DEPOSITS FROM THE LOCAL BANK!
AN ARMORED CAR STOPS HERE EVERY FRIDAY, LIKE CLOCKWORK! DRIVER'S GOT A THING FOR OUR TURKEY SURPRISE!
SO IF WE JUST STAY CALM, LET 'EM TAKE THE CASH--
--I'M SURE THEY WON'T HURT US!
YA GOT A SWEET MOUTH, DARLIN'! KEEP USIN' IT--
--AN' I MIGHT HAFTA SEW IT SHUT!
*

SHE'S NAIVE! FOR THESE MEN TO GET WHAT THEY WANT, *INNOCENTS* WILL BE THE ONES TO PAY!

--BEFORE *SPIDER-MAN* SHATTERED MY LIFE! PERHAPS...

--CALL ON THE ALIEN SYMBIOTE THAT'S JOINED WITH ME-- BECOME *VENOM!*

I WAS INNOCENT MYSELF--

...I SHOULD HELP--

BUT...THAT WOULD REVEAL MY WHEREABOUTS TO THE AUTHORITIES, COMPROMISE MY PRIMARY MISSION:

GETTING TO NEW YORK TO DESTROY *SPIDER-MAN!*

MAYBE THE WOMAN WAS RIGHT. MAYBE NO ONE WILL BE HURT, AS LONG AS--

PUNY LITTLE RUNT, AIN'T HE? PROB'LY GROW UP TA BE A COP!
DON'T TOUCH HIM, YOU SLIMY--
BAD MOVE.
AAGH!
NO!
BLAM
EASY, EDDIE! KEEP CONTROL!
HEY, SMILEY! THIS GUY'S GOT BLACK STUFF ALL OVER HIS FACE!
WHATSA MATTER, PAL?
YER MASCARA RUNNIN'?
WOULD YOU CARE TO STEP OUTSIDE... AND REPEAT THAT?
HEY, SPANGLE! WE GOT OURSELVES A HERO!
RON'S DINER
RON'S DINER
PABLO'S WATCHIN' THE CITIZENS!
LET'S HAVE US SOME LAUGHS!

S DINER
OPEN 24 HRS.
OKAY, SMILEY, YOU PEGGED 'IM --
MAEK
--YOU POUND 'IM!
JUS' CALL ME "MR. SLEDGE!" HEH-HEH--
--HEY! HE WASN'T WEARIN' GLOVES BEFORE!
THNT
KLISH
M-MY WRIST! MY-- EEEAAAAGGH!
KRAK
hmngf?! MRG-GRG!
PLIP

H-HE THREW SOMETHIN' IN SMILEY'S FACE! SMOTHERIN' 'IM!
I'LL BLOW THE SUCKER TO KING-DOM--
PLIP
NO GUNS.
?!
WHRRR-
GUNS HURT!
RAK
OH, MY LORD! B-BLACK GOOP! FLOWIN' ALL OVER 'IM!
WH-WHAT THE DEVIL ARE YOU?!
WE WERE HOPING YOU'D ASK...!

WE'RE CALLED VENOM! AND WE'VE DECIDED TO PLAY THIS GAME--
--BY OUR RULES!
HE'S HIDIN' BEHIND THE RIGS! SPREAD OUT!
B-BUT--!
DO IT!
I KNOW SPANGLE'S THE BOSS--
--BUT THAT GUY IN BLACK AIN'T HUMAN! I-- huh?
D-DRAGGIN' ME UNDER THE TRAILER! T-TOO STRONG--!
HI!
HOW DO YOU LIKE OUR VERSION OF--
--TURKEY SURPRISE!
WHAMP
CHRUNK

NEARBY.
MAYBE SPLITTIN' UP WASN'T SUCH A HOT IDEA! THAT BIG GUY'S WEIRD!
HE COULD BE--
--ANYWHERE?
YOU LIKE TRUCKS?
GOOOOOD!
BECAUSE WE'VE GOT A PRESENT FOR YOU!
OH
NO
SMUSH
HIGH GROUND! ALWAYS A GOOD MOVE! BE ABLE TO SPOT 'IM EASY FROM HERE! ONLY...
...WHERE ARE THE OTHER GUYS?

MAYBE THEY-- WAITASEC!
WHY'S THE LIGHT GETTIN'--
"--BRIGHTER?"
GOTTA JUMP CLEAR! ROLL FREE!
KRRUNP
COME UP SHOOTIN' BEFORE--
YAAAAAH!
KRUNCH
KRUNCH
AWW, DID WE BREAK BOTH OF THEM? Tsk Tsk! AT LEAST LET US GIVE YOUR CIGAR BACK-- OOP!
SMOKING IS BAD FOR YOUR HEALTH!
WE'LL JUST LEAVE IT HERE.
B-BUT... THE GASOLINE--!
NO NEED TO THANK US!
YOUR SMILING FACE IS REWARD ENOUGH!
NO TIME...TO RUN! BUT--
AAAGH! THE PAIN--!
M-MY ARMS! CA... C-CAN'T REACH...
FWOOMB
STRANGERS IN THE NIIIGHT ♫

WHAT THE--?!
FHFFFFFF--
SSHHHOMP
YOU?! B-BUT, HOW--?
THEY GOT CARELESS.
I'M SORRY THIS HAPPENED, CHUCK.
I'M NO DOCTOR, BUT I KNOW A BIT ABOUT SURVIVAL.
FOR WHAT IT'S WORTH, I THINK YOU'LL PULL THROUGH.
BUT I HAVE TO GO. I'VE GOT SOMETHING TO DO, AND I CAN'T HANG AROUND TO ANSWER QUESTIONS. YOU'RE A GOOD MAN, CHUCK.
PROTECTING INNOCENCE IS THE HIGHEST OF GOALS. PROTECTING IT, YES...
SMEK
"...AND AVENGING ITS LOSS!"
END.